Dark Fortune
A Cozy Mystery

Denise Devine
USA Today Bestselling Author

Wild Prairie Rose Books

Dark Fortune

Print Edition

Copyright 2021 by Denise Devine

https://www.deniseannettedevine.com

ISBN: 978-1-943124-31-2

Published in the United States of America

Wild Prairie Rose Books

Cover Design by Raine English

Let's stay in touch!

Sign up for *Denise's Diary*, my monthly newsletter at:
https://www.deniseannettedevine.com/newsletter
You'll be the first to know about new releases, sales and special events.

Passionate about sweet romance?

Want to be part of a fun group?

Visit us on Facebook at:

https://www.facebook.com/groups/HEAstories

Stephanie's Fortune

"I implore you, beware of this warning,

a death occurred before morning.

Your life is in danger, watch out for the stranger,

dark days ahead are dawning…"

Chapter One

James J. Hill Days Celebration

Wayzata, Minnesota

Stood up again…

The pungent aromas of sizzling bratwurst, wood-roasted pizza, and sugary sweet mini-donuts permeated the early evening air, causing Stephanie's stomach to growl as she jostled her way through the dense, interminable crowd of happy festival-goers. She'd planned to arrive an hour ago, but her ride never showed up, forcing her to make a last-minute call to Uber.

Thousands of people attended James J. Hill Days, a tribute to the historic figure who had once owned the Great Northern Railroad in Minnesota and who had built the Wayzata rail depot, now listed on the National Register of Historic Places. The annual event was always held on the first weekend after Labor Day. Tents and trailers housing a unique display of food, retail items, arts, and crafts covered a four-block area of downtown Wayzata along East Lake Street. Country music blared from a large bandshell. As Stephanie passed the vendors selling hot food, her mouth watered at the thought of nibbling on a hot, crispy cheese curd or a pork chop on a stick, but she didn't have time to stop.

She was due to meet the girls in her book club at Main Street

Books tonight at six o'clock for their monthly get-together. Unfortunately, the community celebration underway had drawn so many people, they knew it would be impossible to find a quiet corner in the bookstore for their group of six to congregate. So, they decided to meet as planned and enjoy the festivities instead.

"Watch it, lady!"

In her haste to get to the store, she accidentally bumped into a short, burly man, causing his large, clear plastic cup of craft beer to slosh over his hand. It splashed onto the zippered top of her new shoulder strap purse and dripped down the side. Great. It wasn't bad enough being late, but now she had to deal with a wet, sticky handbag that smelled like beer, too.

It's just one more thing added to the problems I've had today, she thought glumly. *First, Jock doesn't show up, making me late, and now this…*

The red brick building housing Main Street Books loomed in the distance. Stephanie pressed on, maneuvering her way through the crowd until she reached the store. As soon as she opened the door, the bittersweet aroma of fresh-roasted coffee beans surrounded her like a fragrant cloud. To her surprise, she found only three of the girls of the Romancing the Lakes Book Club—Violet, Nora, and Gwen. They were browsing in the romance section.

At least, I'm not the last one to get here.

"Katie had trouble finding a parking space," Gwen said, slipping her phone into her purse, "but she's on her way." Her dark sunglasses were perched on the crown of her head, holding back the thick curls of her chestnut hair.

Stephanie started to explain the reason for her tardiness when suddenly, the glass front doors whisked open and Katie breezed through the crowd, heading straight for the group. "Sorry, I'm late!" Katie's dark hair looked windblown, as though she'd been walking a long way. A couple of strands were twisted around the black, square frame of her glasses.

"I just got here myself," Stephanie said as she dodged a small child charging past her. "This place is a madhouse."

"You're lucky you don't have a car," Katie replied in her usual dry humor and yanked on the hair caught in her glasses. "The parking lot is like a war zone. Did Jock give you a ride?"

"*No.*" Stephanie let out a tense breath. "He was supposed to pick me up from work, but he never showed up and I couldn't get him to return either my calls or my text messages. I finally had to call Uber."

"You should have called me," Katie stated in her bold, matter-of-fact way. "I would have given you a ride."

"I figured you were already here," Stephanie replied, "so it was quicker just to get one on my own."

Katie shrugged, but at the same time, the corners of her lips turned up in a slight curve. "Ah, the continuing saga of your on-again, off-again boyfriend."

Stephanie snorted. "And right now, he's *off* again!" This time, maybe forever. She'd had it with him. He'd stood her up before and each time he'd promised he'd never do it again. So, what had distracted him tonight? A blonde, a brunette, or a redhead?

Though Katie didn't comment further, the look in her eyes said loud and clear, *When are you going to dump that loser? He's not good enough for you.*

At thirty, Jock Tanner wasn't a loser, but even so, he was *far* from perfect. A certified gemologist and jewelry designer, the guy was smart, creative, good-looking, and charming, but he had a tendency to stretch the truth when it suited his purposes and he occasionally changed his plans without telling her. Jock co-owned Majesty Jewelers, a successful jewelry store in downtown Minneapolis, and when the shop was busy, he often had to work late, but that didn't excuse him from not making a quick call or a text to let her know. He couldn't use that excuse tonight, however, because he'd taken the day off. So, where was he?

Her thoughts were interrupted when Inga, the last member to arrive, approached the group. Inga's natural flaxen hair and blue eyes attested to her Scandinavian heritage *and* her beauty. Every male along her path turned in her direction, gazing at her with curiosity as she sauntered through the store. "Am I the last one to arrive?"

The girls chuckled. Inga was *usually* the last one to arrive.

They were discussing where to go from there when someone tapped Stephanie on her shoulder. She turned to find an older, white-haired woman smiling at her.

"I believe you dropped this," the woman said and held out her hand, showing Stephanie a gold hoop earring adorned with four tiny diamonds.

With a gasp, Stephanie automatically reached up and touched her ear. The earring *was gone.* Jock had given the pair to her last month; a peace offering for reneging on an important date. "Oh, my goodness!" She took the hoop from the woman and slipped it back through the hole in her ear, making sure the clasp had fastened tightly this time. "Thank you very much."

"C'mon, Stephanie!" Gwen looked back and waved Stephanie on as she and the rest of the girls strolled toward the front entrance. "We're going to the *Rails and Ales* area to sample craft beers."

Stephanie hurried to catch up with her friends. As she neared the entrance, she saw an older gentleman in khaki slacks, a beige, short-sleeved shirt, and a plain brown bill cap, browsing through a *Field and Stream* magazine. Peering through wire-rimmed glasses, his sharp gaze followed her as she hustled by.

Dirty old man, she thought disgustedly. *Gawk at women your own age...*

They left the store and slowly made their way down the crowded, tent-lined street, stopping at a large food stand to buy mini-donuts. At the bandshell, they watched a rock band pounding out a Guns 'n Roses tune, filling the air with pounding drums and screaming guitars. After that, they browsed along the two-block area of arts and crafts vendors on their way to the beer tents. While the rest of the girls were shopping for handmade jewelry, Stephanie wandered toward a tent selling organic honey and solar-powered lawn ornaments. She loved gardening and was attracted to all things concerning her flowers, especially hummingbirds, butterflies, and bees. She purchased a small set of handmade windchimes and stuffed the bag into her purse.

At the end of the street, they came upon a gypsy wagon. Tucked in between two towering oak trees, the dark brown "cottage-style" coach had a bow top and intricately carved scrollwork in orange and gold covering the front. Above the entrance, a sign hung under a small light that read *Fortune Teller.*

A large wooden A-frame sign on the ground next to the wooden stairway had the word "Palmistry" printed at the top. Underneath, the board displayed a full handprint in dark blue with the words "Know Your Future" printed in the center of the palm in white letters. At the bottom of the sign, she read, "Palm and Eye Readings on Premises." A palm reading cost ten dollars.

"Look," Inga said as she pointed toward the sign. "I've never had my palm read." Her straight flaxen hair slipped past her shoulder as she turned to the girls. "Have you?"

No one else had, either.

Violet pulled a ten-dollar bill from her pocket. "Then let's do it!"

Stephanie stared at the sign in dismay as the girls laughed over what a hoot it would be to have their fortunes told and discussed who would go first.

Are you kidding me? She thought cynically as she stared up at the open café-style doors, beckoning unsuspecting suckers to come into the wagon to get what amounted to a verbal fortune cookie. *What a con. No one can actually tell your future by looking at your hand!*

She turned away and pretended to be busy looking at a display of stained-glass ornaments at a neighboring tent to keep from laughing out loud.

Her friends weren't the least bit skeptical. They enthusiastically discussed the idea while pulling out their money. Inga went in first, then Katie. Each girl took her turn until every person had received her fortune—except Stephanie.

"You're the last one," Katie said to her. "Hurry up. Esme is waiting for you."

"No thanks." Stephanie laughed. "I'll pass. I don't believe in that stuff. Besides, everyone is anxious to check out the craft beers and eat pizza. Let's go." She started to walk away.

"Oh, no you don't!" Katie grabbed her by the shoulders and spun her in the direction of the gypsy wagon. "You're doing this. You need to hear something positive today. Like a prediction that a new man will come into your life tonight."

Stephanie rolled her eyes. *Yeah, right.* Much to her chagrin, she found herself pushed up the steep wooden steps and into the wagon.

"I figured you'd try to weasel out of it, so I've already paid the fee," Katie said with a sly grin, standing behind her. "No need to pay me back." Katie nudged her deeper inside the trailer.

Stephanie stared in amazement as she took in one of the most fascinating micro-homes she'd ever seen. Nothing she'd viewed on cable TV had ever prepared her for this—the arched, gilded ceiling, elaborately carved woodwork, and burgundy velvet drapes. On her right, a tufted velvet bench in burgundy lined the wall. On her left, shiny copper pots placed on a miniature cast iron stove nestled inside a tiled alcove served as a tiny kitchen. In the back of the trailer, fitted from wall to wall, she glimpsed a wide, platform bed covered with a handmade quilt and a small, paned window. Every inch of space was covered with small curio cases and ornate shelving holding crystal glassware, china, framed photos, and unique trinkets. The scent of candle wax and lavender filled the air.

Esme, the raven-haired gypsy sat behind a tiny oval table containing a crystal ball and a stack of Tarot cards. The middle-aged woman wore a white, off-the-shoulder peasant blouse edged with colorful embroidery and elbow-length, bell sleeves. Layers of bejeweled necklaces circled her slender, creamy neck. A burgundy and almond-colored paisley scarf covered the crown of her head.

"Sit down, Miss Jones." She motioned to a wooden folding chair in front of the table. A half-dozen assorted gold bracelets jingled on her narrow wrist.

Stephanie frowned. *How did she know my name? Did Katie tell her?*

Esme's kohl-lined gaze held hers. In the dim light, Stephanie obediently complied as her tension dissipated and an odd sense of calm washed over her. The gypsy made a beckoning motion. "Give me your hand."

Stephanie meekly held out her cold, clammy hand and the woman slid her smooth fingers over it, turning it over. A strange and foreboding stillness filled the atmosphere of the small space as the woman studied her palm. Overhead, the crystals hanging from a glass lampshade began to vibrate, tinkling like wind chimes in the sudden breeze moving through the cabin.

Esme's brows furrowed, her intense gaze locking on Stephanie's eyes. She began to whisper…

"I implore you, beware of this warning;

a death occurred before morning.

Your life is in danger, watch out for the stranger—"

Startled, Stephanie wanted to bolt from her chair. She tried to pull her hand from the gypsy's grasp, but Esme held it tighter. The gypsy leaned closer, looking deep into Stephanie's eyes...

"Dark days ahead are dawning..."

Stephanie sat like one of the statues in the curio cases on the wall, frozen with shock as her mind processed the woman's cryptic advice. *What death? What stranger? What did she mean by 'dark days?' Is it going to storm this weekend or something?*

Slowly, she pushed her chair away from the table and stood then numbly turned away. Gripping the doorframe with both hands, she left the trailer and stumbled down the narrow steps. The sun had gone under a heavy cloud, darkening the sky. The roar of the dense crowd, tinny music from the kiddie carnival rides, and the shrill screams of little riders melted into a blur as she struggled to make some sense of what just took place with the fortune teller.

She had absolutely no idea what this crazy woman was talking about, but even so, she didn't believe a word of it. Warnings and a stupid weather report—what a joke. Katie had just wasted her ten bucks.

* * *

Still dazed from her encounter with the gypsy, Stephanie followed the group toward the beer tents. It was nearly seven o'clock and still not a word from Jock. She pulled her phone from her purse and checked it. Nope; he hadn't called or texted her. Why not? In one of the last messages that she'd left him, she'd told him to meet her at the bookstore as soon as he could get away. She needed to go back to the store one more time to see if he was there. It was probably a waste of time, but...

"I'm going to run back to the bookstore to see if I can find Jock,"

14

she said, catching up to Katie. "Either way, I'll join you guys at the Nordic Brewing tent in a half-hour."

Katie rolled her eyes, conveying what an exercise in futility looking for Jock in this mob would be, but she didn't say so. Instead, she patted Stephanie on the shoulder. "We'll be waiting for you." She cocked one brow. "If you're not there in thirty minutes, you get to buy everyone a beer!"

The girls continued past the kiddie carnival area, heading to the craft beer tents. Stephanie went in the opposite direction toward Main Street Books. She'd made up her mind. She was breaking up with Jock tonight. For good this time. No more on-again, off-again relationship for her. No more leaving her stranded without calling. Her handsome, sweet-talking boyfriend was history.

Under normal circumstances, she could see the log rolling competition on the crystal blue waters of Lake Minnetonka from the street, but not today. The elbow-to-elbow crowd blocked her view. Raucous cheers of an enthusiastic audience watching the event echoed through the air as she made her way back to the entrance of the bookstore.

Preoccupied with angry thoughts, she stepped onto the sidewalk in front of the building, headed toward the glass doors when her wedge-heeled sandal landed on a loose stone causing her ankle to turn. Before she could stop, she lost her balance, and down she went, falling on her hands and knees. *Ouch.*

Oh my gosh! How embarrassing! That's what happens when I'm busy stressing out about Jock instead of looking at where I'm going!

"Whoa, careful there! Are you alright?"

The deep voice booming above her embarrassed her further and angered her for publicly calling attention to her klutzy mishap. It was bad enough almost doing a complete face plant in front of the store but did this jerk with a mouth like a megaphone have to announce it to everyone within earshot too?

"Yes. I'm *fine*." Before she had a chance to scramble to her feet, strong and surprisingly gentle hands spanned her waist, lifting her upright. Averting her gaze, she pretended to be concerned with brushing loose dirt off her ankle-length sundress, hoping to buy a little time to get her emotions under control. Then, with a deep sigh, she turned to face the man, her cheeks burning. "Thanks for your help. I—I was in a hurry and I didn't—"

The man's eyes widened in surprise. "Stephanie? Stephanie Jones?"

She stared into his lean, tanned face, wondering how he knew her because she didn't have a clue to *his* identity. The tall, blond man with thick, curly hair and the bluest eyes she'd ever encountered was a total stranger to her. His voice, however, gave her pause. She could swear she'd heard it somewhere before but couldn't remember where. "Yes..." she replied, studying him intently, "and you are?"

"Shane," he said sounding somewhat mystified that she didn't recognize him. "Shane Kingston."

She blinked, nonplussed. The Shane Kingston she remembered from high school had been gangly and shy, with slick hair, nerdy glasses, and buck teeth. "Wow, you've changed so much I didn't realize it was you."

He grinned. "*You* haven't. You're still as pretty as ever. And you're the only girl I've ever met with your shade of hair. It reminds me of a new penny."

She didn't know why, but his compliment made her cheeks heat up again. "You've...fixed a few things."

He responded with a wide smile, revealing dazzling white— straight—teeth. "I got a summer job in college that offered good insurance. I took advantage of it and got braces. Then I got LASIK surgery so I could get rid of my glasses."

He'd also grown taller and developed muscles in all the right places…

Dismissing that thought, she cleared her throat and changed the subject. She'd had enough trouble with men. The last thing she needed was to get attracted to another one. "I thought you'd moved out of the state. Are you back living here now or just visiting?"

He shoved his hands into the pockets of his jeans, acting as though he had nowhere in particular to go. "I've been living on the west coast for the last ten years, but I'm in between jobs so I'm here visiting my family for a couple of weeks."

"What brings you to the festival?" she asked, hoping he had a date for the evening and had to be on his way.

He glanced over the top of her head as if looking for someone. "I was supposed to meet my cousin, Jock, at the coffee bar in the store at six, but—"

What?

"He was supposed to meet with me, too," Stephanie snapped. "Actually, he'd promised to *bring* me here. It looks like we've both been stood up."

Questions swirled inside her head. Why had Jock agreed to bring her to the festival if he'd already made plans with his cousin? And just where the heck was Jock anyway? Why wasn't he answering his phone?

Shane's tanned face registered surprise. "You're Jock's girlfriend? He's never mentioned you."

Oh, really?

Her cheeks began to burn again, but this time embarrassment had nothing to do with it. She was steaming. "Only for the last twelve months." *Well, off and on…*

"Maybe it slipped his mind," Shane said quickly, obviously trying to spare her feelings. It only made her more upset. He didn't need to make excuses for Jock.

"Sure," she replied dryly. "You know how busy he is…"

This conversation was getting worse by the minute. Getting antsy to be on her way, she checked the screen on her phone. "Oh, look at the time. I'd better get going. I should be sitting with my girlfriends at the *Norway Brewing* beer tent right now instead of wasting my time looking for a guy who doesn't want to be found." Beer wasn't her usual beverage of choice, but right now a glass of cold Viking Blonde Ale sounded pretty darn good. She needed something stronger than Coke to cool off her temper!

"Well, it's been nice seeing you, Stephanie." Shane slid his fingers around her forearm, giving it a gentle squeeze. "Let's not let so many years go by before we meet again. Okay?"

The warmth of his touch made her stomach respond with a strange flutter. What was that all about?

"Okay." She swallowed hard. "See you around, Shane." Puzzled by her reaction, she took a step backward to put some distance between them and lifted her hand, giving him a quick wave of goodbye. Then she whirled around and headed through the crowd, steadfastly making her way across the street.

The golden autumn sun dipped slowly toward the horizon, casting crimson rays across the soft ripples of the bay. Stephanie loved walking along Lake Minnetonka this time of day. She made her way to the bike path that ran along the perimeter of downtown to view the lake on her way back to the *Rails and Ales* area. At the entrance to the bike path, she halted and wistfully gazed across the bay. The balmy evening was so beautiful it would have been nice to take a ride on the lake in Jock's huge boat. That was the only thing about him she was going to miss…

Suddenly, a familiar sight caught her eye. Speaking of Jock's boat—

Glancing to her left, she looked toward the public marina and saw the *Misty Blue*, Jock's cabin cruiser moored at one of the public docks. What was his boat doing here? So, he *was* at the festival and had probably been here all day.

"Why that…" Furious, she marched along, maneuvering in and out of the people on the bike path as she made her way toward the dock. "If he's in there with another woman, I'll…" she grumbled to herself, ready to storm into the cabin and crash their little party. No wonder he wasn't answering his phone; he'd probably turned it off!

Within a couple of minutes, she reached the boat and entered the vessel on the port side. "Jock!" No one answered. "Jock, answer me! I know you're here!"

Several people congregating on the dock curiously turned and stared at her.

The moment her foot stepped onto the cockpit of the boat an unnerving feeling swept over her. An odd, coppery-smelling odor assaulted her senses, sending goosebumps down her arms and raising the hair on the back of her neck. The door to the cabin stood ajar, but not enough to see inside. Had someone broken in and burglarized it?

Gingerly she shoved the cabin door open with the toe of her foot, but she kept her hand on the rail, ready to bolt at the first sign of trouble. "Jock! Are you there?" The cabin was eerily silent. Wondering why Jock had taken off and left the door unlocked, she descended the steps and cautiously peered inside.

Her hand clutched the rail with a death grip to keep her knees from giving way as she blinked in shock. Her jaw dropped. A scream caught in her throat. Across the dim interior of the cabin, Jock lay on his back, sprawled across his bed. A reading light above his head cast enough light to illuminate the deathly pallor of his skin, his black hair, the five o'clock shadow darkening his jaw, and the frozen stare in his open eyes.

A silver filet knife protruded like a vampire stake from the center of his chest.

Chapter Two

The next morning, Stephanie sat on the sofa in her living room, pressing a wadded tissue to her nose. Her mother, Vera, had tucked a stadium blanket around her waist; a wide bed tray covered her lap, holding the cold, uneaten contents of her breakfast. Hobbit, her half-Chihuahua, half-terrier dog, lay next to her, sniffing the air and whining for his self-appointed portion of her food. She hadn't slept—or stopped crying—all night. Vera had tried to encourage her to eat by making bacon, toast, fresh-squeezed orange juice, and scrambled eggs with cheese, but she had no appetite.

"Honey, you need to eat something," her mother said. "It's almost noon." Vera Jones leaned over her and affectionately brushed a lock of hair from her forehead. "I realize it was traumatic finding Jock like that, but it's not helping matters to go all day on an empty stomach." Vera picked up a fork and scooped up a cheese-covered, bite-sized portion of egg. "Here," she said, trying to coax her daughter to eat, "just take a small taste."

Stephanie turned her head away, refusing to try the cold, congealed sampling of her breakfast. "I can't." She squeezed her eyes shut. "I can't stop seeing him lying there...dead. It makes me nauseous."

The horror of finding Jock's body and the subsequent circus of law enforcement personnel crawling all over the scene, inquisitive reporters broadcasting live coverage of the incident, and curious bystanders congregating behind the crime scene tape watching the "breaking news" unfold had been indelibly stamped in her memory, refusing to fade. After giving her statement to one of the officers at the scene, her parents arrived to take her home to her bungalow in a northeast neighborhood of Minneapolis. Vera had stayed with her through the night, holding her hand and keeping her stocked with an ample supply of tissues.

Vera rested the fork on the plate. "I'm so sorry, honey." She had the same jade eyes, coppery hair, and creamy skin as Stephanie, only a more mature version. Vera's straight, chin-length hair held a few strands of gray, but her skin had minimal lines. "Why don't I turn on the television to a Hallmark movie?" She picked up the remote and hit the power button. "That might help take your mind off things."

Ugh.

She loved streaming Hallmark movies and watched them all the time, but she couldn't turn one on today. The last thing Stephanie wanted was to watch a movie with true love and a happy ending—everything she'd always hoped for but had never been fortunate enough to experience for herself. Then she would be *twice* as miserable. Before she could object, the doorbell rang. Hobbit flew off the sofa, barking up a storm.

"I wonder who that is," Vera said and left the living room to answer the door in the narrow front entryway. Overcome with fatigue, Stephanie leaned her head against the sofa's backrest, closing her eyes. Soft voices drifted from the entryway, but she didn't have the energy to make out the words.

A few moments later Vera returned. "There's someone here to see you."

"Oh, Mom, I can't talk to the police again," Stephanie wailed as her eyes opened. "I've already told them everything I know."

"It's not the police." Vera began straightening Stephanie's clothes, fussing over her as if to ensure she looked proper for receiving visitors. "It's a young man." Before Stephanie could object, Vera whirled around and headed to the entryway, signaling to someone. "Come right in."

Heavy footsteps echoed across the polished hardwood floor as the man walked into the living room. Stephanie looked up to find Shane Kingsley standing in front of her. He wore jeans and a long-sleeved t-shirt in blue "acid wash" with a Henley neckline. His thick, blond curls looked more unruly than ever. The rugged, Nordic features of his face were etched with care. "Hi," he said gently, his blue eyes softening as he gazed upon her.

She knew her puffy, red face and bloodshot eyes must look frightful. Some men backed away at the sight of a weeping woman, but if it made him uncomfortable or embarrassed, he didn't show it. "Hi, Shane. Mom, this is Shane Kingsley, Jock's cousin."

Hobbit circled Shane's feet, growling and sniffing the edges of his pant legs.

"Hobbit, come here!" Stephanie scolded as she patted the sofa. He scooted next to her and curled up with his ears perked, his large, liquid eyes riveted on the newcomer. She stroked the smooth, light brown fur standing up on his back to calm his nervous reaction.

Vera brushed invisible lint off one of the twin wingback chairs placed opposite the sofa. "It's nice to meet you, Shane." She gestured for him to sit down. "Would you like some coffee?"

"Yes, please, Mrs. Jones," he said as he obediently took his seat.

Vera disappeared silently into the kitchen, but the smile plastered across her face indicated that she approved of him.

"The police told me you were the person who discovered Jock. It must have been quite a shock. I'm sorry I wasn't there to support you. I left the festival right after I talked to you at the bookstore," Shane said apologetically. "I didn't have any other plans for the night, and I was kind of bored, so I went to the gym for a good workout. I didn't hear about it until my parents called me early this morning. Then the cops knocked on my door, armed with a million questions. I spent the better part of the morning getting interrogated or I would have been here sooner." He leaned toward her. "How are you feeling?"

"Tired." She shook her head. "It doesn't seem real. Finding your boyfriend with a steak knife stuck in his chest. Then suddenly there are screaming sirens and cops swarming all over the place, sealing it off. Last night feels like a bad dream."

His eyes widened. "A steak knife in his chest? Wow…"

She gasped, holding her hands over her mouth. "Oh! You didn't hear that from me, okay? I was told not to divulge the details of the crime scene to anyone."

He nodded. "Don't worry, I won't tell anyone. Your secret is safe with me. I just hope they catch the guy who did it before I have to fly back home."

Vera had left the room but reappeared now with two mugs of coffee, one for her and one for Shane. She set them on the coffee table and motioned for him to take one. She walked over to the other wingback chair and sat down.

Mom, Stephanie thought grumpily, *I'm twenty-five. I don't need a chaperone…*

Shane sat back, stretching out his long legs as he sipped his coffee. "It's all over the news."

Stephanie picked up the remote and shut off her television. A blow-by-blow account of the crime was the last thing she wanted to see. "Do they—do they know who killed him?"

Shane shook his head. "Not yet. An investigator came to my house this morning and asked me a lot of questions, including my whereabouts on Thursday night."

Stephanie swallowed hard. "Is that when Jock…"

Shane nodded. "Around that time, anyway. They didn't tell me if they knew for sure."

"What kind of questions did they ask you?" She wondered why being Jock's cousin automatically made him a suspect.

Shane rested his palms on his knees. He looked so relaxed, but for the life of her, Stephanie couldn't understand why. His cousin had just been murdered! He'd just gone through a grueling interrogation!

"They asked me why I'd come back here from California and about my relationship with Jock," Shane said. "I don't know why because they seemed to know everything about me already, even that Jock had made me executor of his will."

Vera gasped.

You're his administrator? Stephanie thought as she nearly spit out her coffee. *He hasn't seen you in several years. Were you really that close to him?*

"That's why he wanted to meet me last night," Shane followed up quickly. "He said he needed to tell me something important about his will but wouldn't discuss it over the phone."

"I've always known you two were cousins, but I didn't know you and he were that close," Stephanie said.

"We were back when we were kids," Shane replied. "Neither of us has a brother but Jock was like one to me. Our families always did things together like skiing in Colorado and spending weekends during the summer at my parents' cabin up north. Then I took a job on the west coast and our paths diverged. Last Christmas was the first time I'd seen him in five years."

"What did he leave Stephanie?" Vera blurted out.

Oh my gosh, Stephanie thought, mortified that Vera would even mention it. *Jock's estate is the last thing on my mind right now. He doesn't owe me anything.*

Shane must have thought so too as he fidgeted in his chair. He cleared his throat.

Stephanie's coffee cup froze in mid-air, wondering what brought on his discomfort. Perhaps he wasn't allowed to discuss Jock's situation until the reading...

"His will was pretty straightforward," Shane replied simply. "He left his townhome and everything in it to his younger sister, his retirement accounts, the boat, the car, and his half of the jewelry business to his parents."

"What about investments and savings? Didn't he leave anything to Stephanie?" Vera asked.

Stephanie's face heated with embarrassment. "*Mother!*"

"I'm sorry, Mrs. Jones." Shane turned in his chair. "Jock doesn't have any savings or investments. At least, not anymore."

That didn't make any sense. Jock used to call his broker regularly. What happened to his stocks? What happened to his CDs?

Vera's eyes flashed. "He should have left Stephanie something! Hmph! After all, she put up with his nonsense for an entire year."

Well, Stephanie thought, *off and on...*

Uncomfortable with her mother's remarks, Stephanie picked up her fork and busied herself with her breakfast. She was using it as a distraction, but actually, the eggs weren't bad, even though they *were* cold. Hobbit's gaze followed her fork rising from the plate to her mouth. He began to whine for his share. Stephanie fed him a small chunk of bacon to quiet him.

Vera leaned forward in her chair, focusing on Shane. "Are you sure Jock didn't—"

"Mother, would you please refill this for me?" Stephanie held up her half-empty glass of juice. "Thanks."

Vera sprang into action. "Of course." She took the glass and went through the open dining room. "I'm glad to see you're finally eating," she said over her shoulder as she reached the kitchen door. "Clean up that plate!"

Stephanie waited until Vera had stepped safely out of earshot before she spoke. "What do you mean, he doesn't have any savings or investments?" she whispered as she fed another piece of bacon to the dog. "Jock used to brag all the time about how much money he made in the stock market."

"I don't know what happened to any of it," Shane responded with a bewildered look. "It's gone. The investigator said Jock had closed all of his accounts a couple of weeks ago and they wanted to know what I knew about the situation."

Stephanie frowned. "That sounds pretty fishy to me. There's no way he would cash out all of those accounts, and even if he did, where did it go?"

Shane glanced toward the kitchen, making sure he wasn't being overheard. "I don't know, but I have a feeling he may have needed a fast infusion of cash for something."

Stephanie sat back and folded her arms. "That much money was enough to purchase a private plane or a big yacht, but I know he wasn't interested in anything like that. He would have told me about it. And he didn't gamble, so that's out. He could have lost it all on a bad investment, although that doesn't sound like him, either. Where did it go?"

Shane shrugged. "Your guess is as good as mine."

Stephanie heard Vera's footsteps and got busy spreading jam on her cold toast.

Vera returned with a full glass of ice-cold orange juice. "Here you go. It's fresh. I made it this morning." She sat down again. "When is the funeral?"

"No date has been set yet, Mrs. Jones, but I will find out later today," Shane answered politely and sipped his coffee.

Stephanie had a lot more questions to ask him, specifically about what information the investigators wanted, but she knew better than to ask in front of her mother. Vera would turn it into a day-long interrogation.

They spent the next ten minutes talking about the weather and other mundane subjects while drinking their coffee. She sensed Shane had something important he wanted to tell her but couldn't bring it up in front of her mother.

He glanced at the time on his phone and quickly stood. "I'd better get going. I'm meeting Jock's parents at the funeral home at one o'clock to make the arrangements for his memorial service. The autopsy is being performed sometime today and we're told his body should be released within a day or so." He hesitated, his expression grave. "I'm sorry, Stephanie. You should be there, too, but I don't have any control over that. My aunt and uncle requested that only immediate family members be present. The reason I was included is that I'm Jock's executor."

At first, her heart flooded with disappointment, but instead of showing it, she nodded. "Given the way he died, I understand how difficult this situation must be for them. Besides, I barely know them. Jock introduced me to them at a wedding several months ago. They probably don't remember me." Even if she had been invited to attend, she didn't know if she could sit through it without crying her eyes out. She didn't want to cause his family any more discomfort than they were already bearing.

He smiled apologetically. "How about we meet again tomorrow? I'll give you all the details then." They exchanged phone numbers then Shane thanked Vera for the coffee and took his leave.

Stephanie set her tray on the coffee table and stood up to walk him to the door. Hobbit jumped off the sofa and began to yip. "That would be great," she said as she scooped the dog into her arms to quiet him.

She stood at the door to watch him leave, but he paused on the step. "I didn't want to say this in front of your mother," he said in a low voice, "because I didn't want to upset her, but you might be getting a visit from the police. The detective who paid me a visit said he was interviewing everybody."

"Really? I've already told them everything I know…"

Vera came up behind her.

"Thanks for stopping by, Shane," Stephanie said loudly.

"No problem," he replied as he bounded down the steps. "I'll pick you up at six. We'll talk over dinner."

She shut the door and returned to the living room, steeling herself as she caught the curious look in her mother's eye. *It's only dinner between friends, Mother*, she thought with annoyance as she gave Vera a discouraging frown. *Not a proper date.*

She returned to the sofa to think about the events of the past two days and how difficult it was to adjust to Jock's horrible death. It wasn't fair! He was too young to die.

Who did this to him? she wondered angrily. *And why?*

She had just finished drinking the last of her orange juice when the doorbell rang again.

Vera went to answer it with Hobbit on her heels, barking excitedly. Strangely enough, the dog came back almost as quickly as he had left, scurrying faster than before with his smooth tail buried between his legs. He jumped upon the sofa and curled up next to her, snorting his disapproval.

Vera reappeared moments later—pale and shaken—with a stranger following her. "You have another visitor." She placed the empty coffee cups on the bed tray and lifted the tray off the coffee table. "I'll bring this into the kitchen."

The tall, graying man had dark eyes and a dimpled chin. He wore a black suit with a royal blue tie and carried a black vinyl folder. "Good afternoon, Ms. Jones." His deep voice held a serious tone as he held out his credentials for her examination. "I'm Detective Garrett of the Hennepin County Sherriff's office. I'd like to ask you a few questions."

Chapter Three

Stephanie sprung from the sofa, wondering what his visit was all about. "I gave my statement to the officers last night. Have you already gotten a break in the case?"

"No. I need to ask you some follow-up questions," Detective Garrett said in a business-like manner. "My condolences on the death of Mr. Tanner, Ms. Jones," he added quickly, as if anxious to get the formalities out of the way. "I'm sorry to have to bother you at a time like this, but it's routine."

"Mr. Garrett, would you like a cup of coffee?" Vera asked, interrupting him.

"Yes, ma'am, thank you."

She gestured toward the wingback chair Shane had occupied a few minutes ago. "Have a seat." She disappeared into the kitchen.

Stephanie took her previous seat on the sofa and set Hobbit on her lap to keep him quiet.

Detective Garrett sat down and opened his folder to make notes on a lined pad then reached into his pocket and retrieved a pair of slim reading glasses. "I understand from your statement that you were the person who found him." At Stephanie's nod, he slipped on his glasses, clicked his pen, and continued. "What were you doing at the festival?"

"As I told the officer I spoke with last night, my book club meets downtown Wayzata at the bookstore on Friday evening once a month," she replied. "Last Friday was our night to get together, but because of the festival, we decided to visit the *Rails and Ales* area of the event and have some fun instead."

Better not tell him about my incident with the gypsy, she thought as she watched him scribble notes. *It's too weird.*

"Jock was supposed to pick me up after work and bring me to the festival," she continued. "We were going to have a bite to eat before I met up with my book club, but he never showed up, and at the last minute I had to find another ride."

The detective looked up, peering over the rim of his glasses. "Were you upset?"

"Of course, I was." The palms of her hands began to moisten. This sounded more like an interrogation than a *few questions*. "When I saw his boat docked in the bay, I went to confront him about it. I wasn't happy about being stood up and I had planned to break up with him—permanently. I was sick of his broken promises." She kept her voice even, willing herself to remain calm. "This wasn't the first time he'd done that to me."

"How long have you been seeing each other?" the detective asked curiously.

Stephanie stroked the smooth fur on Hobbit's little head. "About a year."

He sketched her answer on his notepad. "How would you describe your relationship?"

Oh-oh. She drew in a tense breath. *He already knows we had more issues than Mars has M&Ms. Someone must have spilled the candy!*

She swallowed hard, worried that her problems with Jock made her a suspect, but she couldn't lie. "To be honest, it was challenging. We broke up a few times."

He looked up again. "Did you know he was seeing another woman?"

"Jock was *always* seeing another woman," Stephanie said. "Every time he got caught, he swore he'd never do it again…but he did anyway. He had a weakness for blondes…"

A dubious expression crossed his face as he stared at her long, coppery hair.

Yeah, she thought dryly. *I have no idea why he kept sweet-talking his way back into my life either. I didn't fit the description of his dream girl…*

Vera returned with a steaming mug of coffee for the detective and a fresh refill for her. As soon as she set them on the coffee table, Stephanie's cell phone rang. Vera snatched it off the coffee table and hurried into the kitchen to answer it.

Detective Garrett grabbed his mug and took a cautious sip. "Do you know of anyone who might be holding a grudge against him?"

"Only about half of the women in this town," Stephanie replied sardonically. "I'm kidding, of course. Truthfully, I have no idea."

The detective didn't seem convinced. "You don't? You just admitted that when he failed to show up last night you suspected he was cheating on you again. That must have made you very angry."

As the man's deep voice rumbled, Hobbit began to shake uncontrollably. He let out a low growl.

"No more than usual." Stephanie placed her hand on the little dog's rigid spine to quiet him. "Look, Jock liked women. They liked *him*. On the surface, his money and his good looks made him seem like quite a catch, but a man who can't keep his zipper up isn't marriage material. I finally concluded that he wasn't going to change—not for me, anyway—and it was time to move on." She shook her head wondering why it took her so long to figure that out herself. "His murder was…an unfortunate coincidence."

Detective Garrett reached into his inner jacket pocket and pulled out a small plastic evidence bag. "Have you ever seen this before?" He held it out for her inspection. It contained an earring composed of a sapphire teardrop stone set in a white gold frame of glittering diamonds.

She nodded. "Yes, I recognize it."

His brows shot up. "Does it belong to you?"

"No," she replied, shaking her head. "It belongs to Jock's store manager, Marsha Goodwin. He made the pair for her as a gift last Christmas. I know because he showed it to me and asked me to gift wrap the box for him." She suddenly realized why he was asking her to verify it. "Did you find it at the murder scene?"

He slipped the bag back inside his coat pocket, ignoring her question. "According to Jock Tanner's partner, Rudy Cohen, the business is missing inventory. Mr. Cohen believes that Jock was skimming diamonds from the store's purchase every time he returned from New York City. Did Jock say anything to you about that?"

She was well aware that Jock made a trip to the diamond district once a month to buy wholesale diamonds. He had a lot of friends in the business in New York City and enjoyed those trips immensely, but he'd never said a word to her about holding back a few diamonds for himself instead of putting them into the company's vault where they belonged.

"No, he didn't," she answered truthfully. Why, then, did Detective Garrett give her the distinct feeling he thought she was lying? "Jock liked to talk about the retail side of his business, but he never delved into the specifics of his financial dealings with me."

Detective Garrett's pen stilled. "Did he ever ask you to store any diamonds for him?"

"No," she declared warily. This conversation was steering in a direction that had become very uncomfortable. "And I wouldn't have agreed to it if he had. Diamonds need to be kept safe in a vault. All I have is a jewelry box."

"But he did give you jewelry as gifts," the detective stated as he sipped his coffee again.

"Of course. Jock gave me jewelry for every occasion." *Especially as a peace offering to get himself out of the doghouse...*

He set down his mug. "May I see your collection?"

"Certainly." Stephanie stood, still holding the dog. Setting Hobbit on the floor wasn't an option. He'd bark and growl non-stop.

Carrying the dog, she led the detective into her bedroom to show him her Queen Anne jewelry armoire. "We'd only been dating a month when Jock gave me this chest with my first necklace," she said as she set the dog on the bed. She reached down to pull open both of the doors, exposing her small, but exquisite collection of pendant necklaces, thick gold chains, and other assorted pieces. "Jock designed everything. He loved creating beautiful things." She shrugged. "It's not exactly what I'd call jewelry, but he gave me a diamond-studded pen, too."

His curiosity apparently satisfied, Detective Garrett pulled off his glasses and stored them back in his jacket pocket. She grabbed the dog as they went back into the living room.

"That's all I have for now. Thank you for your time, Ms. Jones." He handed her a business card. "If you can think of anything else that you might have seen or heard leading up to last night that would help us with the investigation, I'd appreciate a call."

"I will do that," Stephanie promised as she gingerly took the card and shoved it into her pocket. She showed him to the door and came back into the living room when Vera reappeared.

"That was Katie on the phone," Vera said, setting Stephanie's cell phone back on the coffee table. "She called to see how you were doing. She's worried about you. All of the girls are."

"I'll call her back later," Stephanie said as she set the dog on the floor and went into the kitchen. "I'm going outside to water my flowers." The backyard was her sanctuary. Her escape from her problems. No one would bother her there.

*   *   *

I'm done, Stephanie thought wearily as she trooped out the back door. *I can't talk about Jock's murder anymore.*

Hobbit followed her outdoors, sniffing the ground for a place to do his business as Stephanie turned on the outdoor water faucet and pulled the garden hose across the grass. Her backyard wasn't very big, but what it lacked in size it made up for in uniqueness and color. A U-shaped flowerbed bordered with small boulders, solar lights, and yard ornaments defined the back half of her property with a rainbow assortment of annual and perennial plants. She looked around for a suitable place to hang her new wind chimes. Perhaps near the fence…

Mrs. Bona owned the house on the east side of her yard. The elderly widow had lived in this neighborhood for nearly forty years and knew everyone in the area. She knew of all the gossip, too. She kept a close eye on the traffic in the alley and called the police if she saw anything suspicious. Many of Stephanie's neighbors joked that Evelyn Bona's nosiness and hawk-like scrutiny were more reliable than having a security system. True to her reputation, Evelyn presently stood peering through her kitchen window. No doubt she'd gleaned every last detail about Jock's death from the local news and by now the woman probably knew more about the crime than Stephanie did.

Desperate to be alone, she turned on her fan sprayer and began her work. Nothing to see here.

Watering her garden was a calming exercise. After a few minutes, the task always seemed to clear her mind and shift her mood into a feeling of peace, a change she desperately needed today. She exhaled a deep breath, the tension in her shoulders loosening as she turned the fan sprayer on her tall phlox, careful not to bother the bees diligently buzzing from bloom to bloom. The lavender, white, and pink plants grew nearly four feet high and created a natural buffer between her yard and the house on the west side of her that belonged to Valerie Hale. Valerie's sprawling rambler took up nearly all of her corner lot.

An odd feeling prompted her to look up. Stephanie glanced toward Valerie's house and stared through the large windows that wrapped around three sides of the front living room. The tall, exquisite blonde stood nose to nose with her ex-husband, Stuart, embroiled in a discussion. Stephanie knew she shouldn't spy on them, but the curtains were open and curiosity got the best of her.

Valerie, a former model, stood nearly as tall as her ex-husband as she glared into his eyes, her face crimson with smoldering emotion. Since their divorce, she had retired from her career and instead lived off her monthly alimony check. Her ex, Stuart Hale, was a CPA who owned his own firm. He made buckets of money, but he was cheaper than Scrooge. Valerie, on the other hand, was a shopaholic. It didn't take a genius to figure out what they were so worked up about.

I'm so glad I don't have an ex to deal with anymore, Stephanie mused cynically as she redirected the fan sprayer toward a clump of white coneflowers.

Guilt and sadness suddenly overwhelmed her as she realized what had just crossed her mind. She didn't wish for Jock to be *dead*. The thought broke her heart. She squeezed her eyes shut and willed herself to think of something else.

"You've gotten all you're going to get out of me! Understand? The house, the car—it's more than you deserve!"

The loud, acrimonious voice startled her. She moved toward the corner of the house and saw Stuart standing on Valerie's front steps wearing a dark green shirt, the tail hanging out of his jeans. His dark hair, peppered with strands of gray, looked mussed, as though he'd just rolled out of bed. He scowled at her with narrowed eyes.

Valerie pounded her finger in the center of his chest. "I deserve better than this dump, but you don't pay me enough to afford a decent house!"

"Any other woman could afford Buckingham Palace on what you get." He shoved her hand away. "Learn to live on a budget like everyone else!"

He spun away and stomped down the steps.

Valerie followed him to the end of the sidewalk. "We're not finished with this conversation, Stu. You'll be hearing from my lawyer!"

He dismissed her with a wave of his hand as he stormed to his car and jumped in, slamming the door. His vehicle roared to life and sped away.

Stephanie quickly walked back to her garden and continued to water her plants, pretending she hadn't heard a thing—and hoping Valerie was so preoccupied she didn't notice anything else. Within a few moments, however, the familiar swish-swish of a woman's footsteps tripping through the grass indicated Valerie was heading her way.

"He makes me so mad!" Valerie proclaimed loudly as she approached. "Did you hear what that jerk said to me?"

There goes my temporary escape from reality, Stephanie thought dismally. She slowly pivoted. Valerie wore an aqua knit top and a pair of white chinos. The tapered, ankle-length pants accentuated her tall, slender figure. The low-cut top barely covered her ample bosom. "Hi, Val."

"He thinks I should be grateful for that paltry allowance he dols out every month," Valerie spouted as her full lips formed a well-rehearsed pout. Her shoulder-length hair had been hastily swept to the crown of her head in a messy bun. She folded her arms into a tight bow. "When my lawyer gets him in court, he'll wish he'd played nice with me!"

Hobbit barked and did his usual happy dance to see her. "Behave yourself," Valerie scolded him and waved her hand to shoo him away. "You're going to get mud on my clothes."

Stephanie ignored Hobbit's bad manners and went back to tending to her flowers, hoping Valerie would get a clue that she didn't want company and go home.

"I saw the report about Jock on the news," Valerie said, taking a softer tone. "How are you doing?"

Stephanie winced at the question but replied, "I'm okay. I just need some quiet time to deal with the shock." *Hint, hint.*

"It's too bad he wasn't the marrying kind of guy," Valerie stated boldly. "You'd be sitting pretty right now."

Leave it to Valerie to think about Jock's net worth at a time like this!

"I have everything I need," Stephanie stated, her patience wearing thin. "Right now, I'm more concerned with *why* he died than who is inheriting his estate."

"Is this new?" Valerie pointed toward a shallow bowl of pebbles hanging by three slim chains from a black metal shepherd's hook.

"No, I've had it since last spring," Stephanie replied, happy to change the subject. "Jock gave it to me for my birthday. It's been hanging there in my flowerbed all summer."

Valerie curiously picked one of the multi-colored pebbles out of the bowl and examined it. "What is it for?"

"It's a bee bowl."

Valerie laughed. "A what?"

"It's a bowl for bees and butterflies to drink water. It comes as a kit. Jock set it up for me." Stephanie pointed toward the blue ceramic dish. "You cover the bottom with pebbles and fill it with an inch of fresh water. The bees and butterflies can sit on the rocks and safely get a drink without drowning."

"How ironic," Valerie said in a droll voice as she examined the small nugget in her palm. "The man is rolling in precious stones and he gives you *this*…"

Stephanie shrugged. "It's what I wanted." She refreshed the dish with a small amount of clean water. "I have enough diamonds."

Valerie snorted with incredulity. "Honey, a girl *never* has enough diamonds."

"Jock knew how much my garden means to me," Stephanie said with a sniff. "He wanted to get me something special so he asked me to pick out my favorite things at the garden center. Sometimes he could be really sweet. At other times…"

Valerie frowned at the light pink pebble and tossed it back into the bowl. "Sometimes I regret introducing you to him."

Stephanie gasped, taken aback by Valerie's directness. "Why would you say such a thing?"

Valerie placed her hand on Stephanie's arm, her face reflecting concern. "Don't take this the wrong way, but Jock wasn't right for you."

"What do you mean?"

"He cheated on you every chance he got," Valerie said solemnly. "It was obvious he never loved you."

Deep down, Stephanie had always known the truth, but to hear Valerie say it out loud pierced like a shard of glass through her heart. She turned away to conceal her tears and in the process her foot caught on the hose, pitching her forward. The fan sprayer flew out of her hand.

"Ah-h-h!" Valerie screamed as cold water sprayed across the front of her body, drenching her from head to toe. "Stephanie! What are you doing?" She backed up, furiously trying to shake the water from her eyes. "Oh, my gosh—I'm soaked. What if someone sees me like this!"

"I'm sorry, Val," Stephanie called out. "It was an accident!"

Either Valerie hadn't heard her or she'd refused to answer as she stomped back home.

Every time I get stressed out, I trip on something, Stephanie thought miserably. Deciding she'd had enough gardening for one day, her feet automatically headed for the outdoor faucet. *It's been that way all my life,* she complained silently to herself. The handle squeaked as she turned off the water. *How am I going to make it through Jock's funeral in one piece?*

She shuddered at the thought. The last thing she needed was to crash and burn in the funeral home and wipe out Jock's memorial in front of God and everybody...

Chapter Four

On Monday morning, Stephanie arrived late for work at Chloe's Couture, a fashion boutique in the Hennepin Avenue/Lake Street area in Minneapolis called Uptown. The stressful weekend had left her tired and not at all in the mood to deal with customers. The shop had been open for ten minutes by the time she clocked in.

Last Saturday evening, her weekend had taken a disappointing turn when Shane called and cancelled their dinner plans for Sunday. He apologized, explaining that he wasn't aware his parents had already made their own plans for him. They wanted him to drive up north with them to their cabin in Bemidji to help pull in the dock and close up the house for the winter. He said he wouldn't be back home until sometime Monday afternoon but promised to pick her up for dinner on Monday night instead. Before he hung up, however, he mentioned the funeral service for Jock would be at seven on Wednesday evening at The Blacklock Funeral Chapel and said he'd fill her in on the other details over dinner.

Monday was usually a slow day for business, but Stephanie passed the time by marking down close-out items and organizing them on the sale rack at the back of the store. After that, she unpacked a box of blouses. Anne, her coworker, had gone back to their small breakroom to eat her lunch, leaving Stephanie to run the shop alone for a half-hour. She stood in front of the garment steamer refreshing a blouse when the door chime indicated someone had entered the shop.

She squared her shoulders and put forth her sunniest smile as she made her way to the front of the store, hoping the customer didn't stay long. "Good afternoon. May I help you—"

Taken by surprise, she stopped short. Marsha Goodwin, the manager of Jock's store, Majesty Jewelers, stood in front of the sales counter gripping her leather clutch purse with both hands. The tall, thirty-something woman had a slender figure and straight, elbow-length blonde hair with a center part. She was a regular customer but today, the icy stare in Marsha's wide amber eyes indicated she had no interest in shopping for additions to her wardrobe.

Stephanie rested one hand on the glass counter to steady herself. "Hello, Marsha." Beyond that, she didn't know what else to say.

"This is all *your* fault," Marsha announced in a breathy, ultra-feminine voice. Everything about her exuded the image of someone who wanted everyone to believe she came from wealth and privilege—from her blush pink designer dress in silk crepe and matching stiletto sandals to the dazzling diamond ensemble accenting her ears, neck, and wrist. "You've been nothing but a pain in my side for an entire year and now that Jock's gone, you've permanently ruined my life!" Her gaze swept over Stephanie with disdain. "You, of all people!"

Stephanie let out a tense breath feeling like Alice in Wonderland standing before the Queen of Hearts. Marsha had never made any attempt to conceal her jealousy over Stephanie's relationship with Jock. The woman definitely possessed the look that Jock found attractive, but her type—*an arrogant, demanding princess with an air of entitlement*—never kept him interested for long.

"Thanks for the compliment," Stephanie said dryly. "What do you want?"

Marsha moved closer, her eyes narrowing. "I want the diamonds that Jock gave you to stash somewhere for him. All of them. If Rudy doesn't get them back, he's going to close the store and I'll lose my job. I know you have them and you'd *better* give them up." She thrust out her hand adorned with a large sapphire and diamond ring. It matched the earring that Detective Garrett found on the boat. "To me!"

"That's not true," Stephanie said, annoyed that Marsha would accuse her of such dishonesty. "I know only that they're missing from the vault because Detective Garrett told me about it. Nothing more. *If* Jock took them, he never confided in me about it."

"You're lying." Marsha glared at her with a condescending sneer. "I can see the truth plainly in your eyes. You probably think you've got the perfect plan to get rich quick but you're not smart enough to sell them on the black market so don't even try. If you so much as contact a prospective buyer, I guarantee you'll be arrested." She pointed a long, expertly manicured pink nail at Stephanie. "For your information, Detective Garrett is on to you. I told him all about how you manipulated Jock into coming back to you every time he broke up with you. Thanks to me, Garrett knows what a conniving, fortune-hunting witch you are!"

"Like I said, I don't know anything about the diamonds, but I'm sure Rudy had them insured. And just to set the record straight on another point, Jock never broke up with me," Stephanie countered. "I broke up with *him* but he always came back begging for another chance."

Marsha responded with a haughty laugh. "How'd that work out for you?"

Tired of this pointless confrontation, Stephanie folded her arms. "I have nothing more to say to you. Goodbye."

Instead of leaving, Marsha leaned closer. "Well, I have something else to say to you. Your doting boyfriend and I went to New York City every month. We dined together, went to Broadway shows together…" Her brows arched. "We *made love.*"

Stephanie didn't know if Marsha was telling the truth or if the vindictive twit was just looking for a way to get even with her for denying she had the diamonds, but at this point, why did it matter? Jock was dead. She had planned to break up with him last Friday, so Marsha's claims didn't cut her as sharply as the woman had intended, but the need to win this argument ran deep.

"So, you were his weekend entertainment," Stephanie retorted. "How'd that work out for *you*?"

Marsha's face turned crimson. Her nostrils flared.

Aha, Stephanie thought victoriously, *that hit a nerve.*

"Jock loved me," Marsha cried. "We were going to get married!"

"Then you've been jilted," Stephanie declared. "The last time we mended our relationship he gave me a gift that proved how much he wanted me back."

Marsha's pink, full-lipped mouth gaped open. "A ring?"

A pen, Stephanie thought sadly, *a rare diamond-encrusted pen.*

"That's between him and me," she said with finality.

"I knew it," Marsha shot back, her voice dropping to a hiss. "You're basically admitting he gave you a cache of diamonds to hide for him. Detective Garrett will be very interested in hearing about this!" She spun around and began to walk quickly toward the entrance. At the glass door, she stopped and looked back. "Did you kill him?"

The question caught Stephanie off guard at first. Then it incensed her. "No!" Stephanie gripped her hands on her hips and glared at the woman. "Did you?"

Refusing to answer, Marsha jerked open the door and stormed out, her stiletto sandals pounding a sharp click-click-click on the pavement as she disappeared.

Stephanie collapsed into the nearest chair, exhausted and

wondering what Marsha meant when she said Detective Garrett was 'on to her.' Did Marsha's assertion mean he had assigned someone to follow her with the expectation that she'd lead them to the stolen merchandise?

"But I don't have them," she wailed in frustration. "I don't know anything about them."

She fought back the urge to shed tears of self-pity, wishing she'd never heard of Jock Tanner.

*   *   *

That afternoon, Stephanie took the bus home from work, as usual. A monthly rider pass on the bus was much cheaper than owning a car and it was fairly convenient; the nearest stop was only a half-block away from her residence. As soon as she entered her living room, she kicked off her leather high-heeled sandals and stepped out of her flowered dress. Then all of her jewelry came off, including her favorite three-tiered emerald and diamond ring, a birthday present from Jock. Shane wasn't due to pick her up for another twenty minutes, giving her some time to visit the backyard and give her flowers a good watering. She changed into a comfortable pair of burgundy denim leggings with a matching top in flowing georgette, slipped on a worn pair of Crocs, and headed out the back door.

Though it was mid-September and the trees were beginning to turn color, the weather continued to be summer-like with warm, sunny days. The temperature had reached the high 70s today and many of her flowers were still blooming.

"Hobbit! No!" She yelled as her pooch lifted his leg and urinated on the corner of the house. She rolled her eyes in disgust then turned on the hose and showered the cream-colored stucco with plenty of water to wash off the stain. Oblivious to his faux pas, Hobbit began to chase a butterfly.

"Oh, Stephanie!" Evelyn Bona stood at the white picket fence dividing their properties on the west side in a light blue checkered housedress and holding a vintage Tupperware container. The stout, white-haired woman held out the item, yellowed with age, as Stephanie dropped the hose and walked to her side of the fence. "I've made you an apple pie."

"That sounds wonderful. Thank you," Stephanie said happily as she accepted the pie-taker. "Gosh, it's still warm."

Two years ago, she'd qualified for a first-time homebuyer loan from the City of Minneapolis, enabling her to purchase her house. She met Evelyn as soon as she moved in and since then, the woman had been like a grandmother to her.

"I thought you could use some cheering up." Evelyn kissed her cheek. "Sweetie, I'm so sorry to hear about Jock. I didn't get home from Eau Claire until late last night, but I saw it on the news this morning. How are you doing? Is everything okay?"

"As good as it can be." Stephanie swallowed hard to keep her emotions in check. "Everyone has been so kind."

"Hmph! *Nearly* everyone." Evelyn gestured toward Valerie's beige rambler on the opposite side of Stephanie's yard. "I saw what happened last night between you two. Typical Valerie. I didn't blame you for spraying her with the hose. At least it shut her up!" Evelyn shook her head. "I was tempted to step outside and tell her to mind her own business."

And it would be just like Valerie to overhear us right now and come over here to make a stink about it... Stephanie thought guiltily as she glanced around. Things were bad enough between her and Valerie right now. She didn't need more unpleasantness.

"Val is one of the most self-centered women I've ever known. Beware of her," Evelyn said with disgust. "She's a conniver. I wouldn't trust that woman as far as I could shove her." Stephanie's face must have given away her shock because Evelyn's white brows arched in her own defense. The look in her brown eyes indicated she was dead serious.

"I've seen some things…" She paused as if weighing what to divulge. "Like the way she tries to manipulate Stu into giving her more money by coming on to him—slipping his shirt off and pulling him into the bedroom."

Stephanie gasped. Yikes! Evelyn made Valerie's love life sound like a steamy daytime soap opera. Too much information!

"Well, it's true…" Evelyn guffawed. "She leaves her shades wide open like she's performing for an audience!"

The last thing Stephanie wanted to do was discuss what went on between Valerie and Stu with Evelyn. Anxious to change the subject, she suddenly developed a serious interest in the contents of the pie-taker. "I've got a few minutes to spare before my ride is due. Maybe I'll treat myself to some pie and ice cream right now."

As if on cue, a black Lincoln Navigator rolled up to the curb, parking on the street between their houses.

"There's my ride," she said, relieved. "He's early." She waved to Shane as he climbed out of Jock's SUV. He took the narrow sidewalk along the side of her house and headed toward the backyard wearing snug jeans and a blue plaid shirt.

"My, but he's quite a looker," Evelyn said with a chuckle. "He reminds me of Bo in the Dukes of Hazzard."

"Sh-h-h, he'll hear you," Stephanie whispered, embarrassed to her toes. Evelyn's favorite pastime was watching a local station that showed only vintage television shows, but why she watched *that* old TV series about scantily clad girls and fast cars was anybody's guess.

Shane opened the gate in the picket fence and let himself in. Hobbit must have decided he liked the guy because this time he jumped against Shane's pant leg and barked with glee. "Hi," Shane said, focusing on her as he petted the top of the dog's head. He gave her a shy smile and pointed to the pie-taker. "Whatcha got there?"

"Shane, this is my neighbor, Evelyn. She made me an apple pie." Stephanie held it out. "Want a piece?"

He greeted Evelyn with a wide grin then shoved his keys into the pockets of his jeans. "Sure, but why don't we go out for dinner first? We can come back here afterward and have it for dessert."

"Okay," Stephanie said as she hurried toward the house, eager to get going. "I'll put this in the kitchen, get the dog squared away, and meet you at the car." She waived to Evelyn. "Thanks so much for the pie, Evelyn. Bye!"

She put the container on the counter and grabbed a can of dog food from the pantry. Hobbit got his usual tablespoonful of wet food in his dish as a treat. After he took care of his potty business outdoors, she grabbed her purse, locked the door, and left the house.

She was anxious to find out if Shane had learned anything new about Jock's murder from the Tanners.

Chapter Five

Eager to talk to Shane, Stephanie slipped into the cool, luxurious interior of the SUV and shut the door. "Where are we going?"

Shane slipped on his sunglasses, pulled away from the curb, and drove slowly down the block. "Someplace private. Where we can converse freely without worrying about anyone overhearing us."

Oh, my gosh, Stephanie thought, surprised. *He must have something important to share that's for my ears only. Now I really want to know what's going on.* She studied him, wondering what was going through his mind. Had he learned something new about Jock's murder and was trying to figure out how to break it to her? She folded her hands in her lap and waited for him to fill her in on the details.

Instead of talking about Jock, however, Shane switched on the radio and turned the volume down low. He glanced her way. "Do you like old-fashioned root beer in a frosted mug?"

"Yeah." She smiled. "On a day like today, it hits the spot."

"Great." He smiled back but didn't say anything else.

She set her purse by her feet and sat back, getting comfortable in the soft leather seat. "How did your appointment turn out at the funeral home on Saturday?"

"Jock had a lot of business associates so my aunt and uncle are expecting a large crowd," Shane replied. "The obituary is online and it's probably in today's paper as well." He sounded sad, revealing how much he already missed his favorite cousin. "He's being cremated today so there won't be a viewing for him."

"That's what Jock would want," Stephanie said somberly. "Yes, I saw it in the paper. His parents published a large piece about him. I called my friends and they're taking me out for dinner before we go to the service. Katie is going to pick me up."

It seemed so strange to be referring to Jock's funeral. And so difficult to grasp. The thought made her profoundly sad, especially for his parents.

Shane went quiet again. He seemed preoccupied with something. She wanted to know what was wrong but thought it would be rude to ask about it. It would sound like she was trying to pry into his business. Instead, she kept herself busy staring out the window until they pulled into an old drive-in restaurant, now restored to look like it did back in its glory days in the 1950s. The small, square building with a bright neon sign on the roof was attached to a long canopy with a dozen stalls underneath it for cars to park in the shade and order food. A wide serving counter ran parallel to the building where people could sit outdoors and enjoy their meal in the fresh air. Behind the building, a couple of children were chasing each other around a playground area containing swings and a sandbox. Off to one side was a mini-golf course. Fifties rock music, lively and loud, penetrated the air. The idyllic scene was just the sort of place where they could forget all that was going on for a while.

Stephanie looked around, wide-eyed. "This place is really cool. To tell you the truth, I didn't know it existed."

Shane pulled into one of the stalls next to an older couple in a blue and white 1957 Chevy that looked like it had just been driven off the showroom floor. "My dad used to bring me here when I was a kid.

It's still operated by the family of the original owners. They serve the best burgers I've ever eaten."

They unlatched their seatbelts and scrutinized the menu then ordered burger baskets and mugs of old-fashioned root beer through the speaker on the menu board next to the driver's side window. Knowing it would be a while before they received their food, Stephanie relaxed again and wondered what Shane had to say about the investigation. She needed to know what was going on.

Before she could ask, a "carhop" with long brown hair pulled into a ponytail approached the car window wearing saddle shoes, a cashmere sweater, and a pink poodle skirt. The teen carried a metal tray holding two root beer mugs and a stack of napkins. She hooked it on Shane's partially lowered window and handed him the receipt. Shane pulled off his sunglasses and set them on the dashboard then grabbed his wallet. He pulled out a couple of bills to pay for their food, telling the girl to keep the change.

"I got an interesting phone call today," he announced as he handed a cold, frosted mug to Stephanie. "The guy said he was an accountant who was hired to perform an audit to determine Majesty Jeweler's financial situation."

She took a couple of refreshing sips of her root beer and rested her mug on the wide console between them. "What did he want?"

"The second half of his fee," Shane said in a serious tone. He grabbed the other mug and took a generous gulp of the dark frothy soda.

Puzzled, she shifted in her seat, facing him. "Why did he call you? Jock's bookkeeper is the person who he should have called—or did she refuse to pay it?"

"His bookkeeper doesn't know about it. Neither does Rudy," Shane said and took another swig of his root beer. "According to the accountant, Jock had made a private arrangement with him." He gave her a sideways glance. "Jock was working with the guy on the sly while the bookkeeper was on vacation. He wanted to know if Rudy was cooking the books."

Stephanie stared at him, stunned by this new revelation. "Was he?"

Shane nodded.

"How?"

"Rudy has been charging thousands of dollars every month to his expense account, for one thing," Shane replied. "He's also been drawing out large amounts of cash for miscellaneous expenses, but as the saying goes, that's just the tip of the iceberg. While he's attempting to throw suspicion on Jock for poaching diamonds from their inventory, Rudy's been doing his share of robbing the till himself. Given the way things are going, in a few months, the store will be bankrupt."

Stephanie picked up her mug and placed a napkin under it to prevent the melting frost on the glass from dripping on her lap. "So, Jock suspected something was going on with Rudy and he decided to get proof in writing." She gasped. "That makes Rudy a suspect."

"Sure does," Shane said wryly. "And that's not all. The store was paying the premiums on huge life insurance policies for both Rudy and Jock. They designated each other as the prime beneficiary so if anything happened to one of them, the other would have a nice down payment to buy out the deceased partner's family. And get this—" His brows shot up. "It was Rudy's idea."

Stephanie drew in a sharp breath. "Oh, my gosh…"

Shane nodded in agreement. "I'm meeting with the accountant tomorrow to pay the final payment out of Jock's personal funds and to collect the evidence. Then I'm going to turn it all over to Detective Garrett. I have an appointment with Mr. Hale at noon for lunch."

The mention of that name caused her to nearly choke on her root beer. "Are you talking about Stuart Hale?"

Shane frowned. "Yeah, you know him?"

"He's my neighbor's ex-husband," she replied. "Valerie Hale's house is the one on the corner. I saw him yesterday as a matter of fact. He and Val were having one of their frequent, not-so-friendly discussions about the size of her alimony payments."

"So, Jock and Stuart Hale were friends," Shane said quietly, pondering aloud. "I wonder how much this guy really knows about the relationship between Rudy and Jock."

"Probably a lot," Stephanie replied enthusiastically. "They've known each other for a long time. Stu and Val introduced me to Jock at a party at their house back when he and Val were still married." She stared out the windshield, observing a couple of boys playing mini-golf. "The embezzlement piece is going to make settling Jock's estate a lot more complicated, isn't it?"

He set his empty mug on the tray and let out a sigh. "Yeah, but I don't have that much time to devote to it. I have to get back to California soon."

"I imagine you do," Stephanie said sympathetically. "Gosh, we've had so much going on that I've never had a chance to ask you what you do for a living."

He rested his hand on the steering wheel. "I work in the motion picture industry as a stunt double for Dack Reynolds. We're scheduled to start on our next film in a couple of weeks."

Her jaw dropped. "Wow," she said, stunned. Dack Reynolds was a Hollywood megastar whose action films often broke box office records. "I'll bet that's exciting—"

"It's not a nine-to-five job and at times it can be risky, but that's why I love it," he said with a grin. "It's different and challenging every day."

"How did you get interested in working in movies—if I may

ask?"

His grin widened. "As a kid, I was obsessed with action films and watched everything I could get my hands on. By the time I was ten years old, I knew what I wanted to be when I grew up."

"Really?" Given that the Shane she knew in school was extremely shy, she found his story amazing. "What's your favorite movie?"

"Terminator," he said, sounding like Arnold Schwarzenegger, "Star Wars, Matrix, the original Mad Max."

She laughed. "I've seen a couple of Dack's movies and it's hard to imagine that he isn't the one climbing out of burning cars or flying through the air on a motorcycle. You're very good at what you do." She stared at his profile as she compared his lean square jaw and the thick, blond curls covering the nape of his neck to the movies she'd seen of Dack Reynolds. "I can see why you pass for him." Her gaze traveled to his muscular arms. "From even a short distance you could easily be mistaken for him."

He turned her way and slung one arm across the back of his seat. "I'm not like him in any other way, though. He's a hero in front of the camera, but in private, Dack is arrogant, foul and he treats women like dirt under his feet." Shane took his free hand in hers as he stared deeply into her eyes. "I'm still the same guy you knew in school."

Her heartbeat sped up a notch. *Not really,* she thought. *You're much more mature and self-confident than the kid I used to know.*

He must have read her thoughts for he gave her a knowing look and took his hand away. "It's easy for me to perform as Dack's double because no one knows it's me." He laughed. "But don't ask me to get up in front of a crowd and give a speech. I'll start stuttering and make a fool of myself."

"Really?" she replied, amazed. "That's me, too. Only I wouldn't just stammer. I'd probably trip over my own feet and topple the podium."

That got a laugh out of him, but she could tell he wasn't taking her answer seriously.

"I mean it," she argued. "Don't you remember picking me off the pavement at the festival?"

"Come on," he countered skeptically. "That wasn't your fault. It was an accident."

"Maybe so, but it wasn't the first time I've crashed and burned. I was so upset over Jock not picking me up from work that I failed to pay attention to where I was going. It was so embarrassing falling on the sidewalk in front of the bookstore!" Becoming upset about it all over again, she looked down at her lap. "It happens sometimes when I get distressed."

He slipped his finger under her chin and lifted her face. "Then I guess we're both still just a work in progress."

Their gazes met and held. Something in her heart stirred.

"Here you are, sir." The carhop stood outside the window and placed their burger baskets on the tray along with plastic squirt bottles containing ketchup and mustard. "Would you like another root beer?"

"No thanks," Shane said. "Could I trouble you for a glass of water instead?"

He turned to Stephanie and handed her a red plastic basket lined with red and white checkered paper and filled with a huge burger and fries. "Would you like one, too?"

She held up her mug. "I still have half of my root beer."

The carhop left to fetch his water, leaving them to start on their burgers.

"Marsha Goodwin came into the shop today," Stephanie said as she squirted a mound of ketchup next to the fries in her basket. She picked up her juicy burger stuffed with cheese, lettuce, tomato, pickle, and a special sauce, holding it with both hands to keep it from falling apart. Thankfully, the bun was toasted nice and crisp, making the sandwich more stable. "She's Jock's store manager."

"I know who she is," Shane replied. "I met her the other day when I went into the store to see Jock. What did she want?"

Stephanie took a bite of her burger and groaned. "Oh, this is good."

"Told ya," Shane said with his mouth full.

She swallowed and blotted her hand against a napkin as a stream of sauce dripped from the burger and ran down her wrist. "Marsha accused me of stowing the diamonds for Jock and holding out on the police. And…" She interrupted herself to take another bite of her luscious dinner. After a short pause, she continued. "She told me that Jock was in love with her. That they spent weekends together in New York City when he went to the diamond district." She stared at her basket, barely able to get the last sentence out. "She said they were going to get married."

Shane looked up from his food. "I doubt that. She's not his type."

Stephanie picked up a crispy fry and dipped it into a mound of ketchup. "She's the type he always chased after when he cheated on me. Marsha is a smart, classy, beautiful blonde."

Shane responded with a chortle. "She's a high-maintenance nightmare—"

"—and so much more sophisticated than me."

He held up his burger to take another bite but stopped. "She has *nothing* on you, Stephanie. You want to know why Jock kept coming back to you? Because you're sweet and genuine. Someone he knew he could trust. The kind of girl a guy is proud to take home to meet his parents."

He didn't trust me enough, she thought sadly. *And he didn't take me home to get better acquainted with his parents, either.*

"*If* he had trusted me," she declared, "he wouldn't have kept the truth about the diamonds from me."

Shane picked up a large fry and pointed it at her. "Maybe he was trying to *protect* you."

"Maybe," she replied glumly, "but if he was, it backfired on both of us. Everybody suspects me of colluding with him—even Detective Garrett. He didn't say as much, but I could tell by the questions he asked that he thinks I know more than I'm telling. A lot more."

Shane grabbed a napkin and wiped his hands. "Everyone is a suspect right now. Even me."

She sighed and set her burger basket on the dashboard. "I wish I knew where Jock hid those diamonds he supposedly stole from the store. If I did, I'd give them back."

Shane studied her for a few moments, as though deep in serious thought. He arched one brow. "Why don't you and I start searching for them?"

His hopeful smile faded to a frown of disappointment when she shook her head in refusal.

"I wouldn't know where to start," Stephanie argued. "I mean, the cops have been all over Jock's house and business. If they couldn't find the diamonds, I don't see how we could."

Even so, a still, small voice whispering in the back of her mind warned her not to give up so easily.

Chapter Six

Stephanie had Wednesday off, providing her plenty of time to get ready for the service. She dressed in Jock's favorite outfit, a simple black chemise with three-quarter-length sleeves, a black clutch, and her best designer pumps then dabbed a drop of Coco Mademoiselle behind each ear. To honor his unique artistic gift, she decided to wear the emerald and diamond set he had given her on her birthday. The pendant necklace held a one-carat stone, emerald cut with a white-gold chain. Round and baguette diamonds framed the magnificent jewel. Jock had paired it with drop earrings and a matching ring.

She put on the beautiful set and stared at the dazzling pendant in the mirror, remembering the night Jock had given it to her. He'd surprised her with a black velvet box during dessert at their favorite restaurant and when she opened it, he said he'd designed the set to compliment the feature about her he loved the most—the thick, curly tresses of her shining copper hair.

Before she could catch it with her finger, a tear slipped from her eye and ran down her cheek. *Think about something else or you'll be a mess by the time Katie arrives*, she thought as she reached for a tissue. *You just spent twenty minutes putting on your makeup. You don't have time to wipe it all off and start over—*

The doorbell rang. Hobbit chimed in, barking excitedly, as though he knew whose finger was pressing on the bell. She blotted her eyes and swallowed back her sadness as she made her way through the house to answer it.

"Yes, Hobbit, I can hear you," Katie said as she crossed the threshold and reached down to pet the whining dog. "No need to get yourself worked up now." She reached into her purse. "Here's your treat. See? I didn't forget."

Hobbit grabbed the huge milk bone and ran toward the bedroom to chew on his treasure in private, his nails tapping rapidly on the hardwood floor.

"Well," she said, straightening, "now that we have the necessities out of the way, we can get going." She wore black slacks and a matching blazer with a deep burgundy blouse. Her dark hair fell in soft curls about her shoulders. She adjusted her black-framed glasses and checked her watch. "It's four on the nose. If we leave now, we won't have to rush. We can take our time at dinner and still get to the chapel in plenty of time for the service."

Stephanie grabbed her purse and a light coat. "I already let the dog out to do his business so he's fine." She marched toward the door, but Katie stopped her.

"How are *you* doing?" Katie slipped her arm around Stephanie's shoulder. "Are you okay?"

"Yeah," Stephanie said with a long sigh. "I'm so sad about what happened to Jock, but I'm going to say goodbye to him tonight and get on with my life."

"Good! You're doing the right thing," Katie replied enthusiastically. "Come on, we're supposed to meet the girls in fifteen minutes at Pedro's Cantina for enchiladas."

The thought of a fizzing Coke over ice and a hot, cheesy

enchilada made her mouth water. "Great!" She locked the door behind her and followed Katie to the car.

Violet, Nora, Inga, and Gwen were already seated and munching on chips and salsa by the time they arrived at the cantina. Everyone greeted her with a hug and told her how sorry they were about Jock's passing, even if he hadn't been their favorite person after the way he had treated Stephanie. Nora passed around a sympathy card for Jock's family. Each person signed it and passed it on to the next one while they waited for their food to come. Stephanie had prepared one as well for the family earlier that day and had it stowed in her purse.

After dinner, they drove to the funeral chapel, arriving in plenty of time for the service. They walked into a wide reception area decorated with sea green carpet and draperies, cream walls, and ornate furniture. Stephanie and Nora dropped their cards into the memorial box as each girl signed the guest register. An elbow-to-elbow crowd of people filled the huge facility, many of whom were strangers, but Stephanie recognized all of Jock's business colleagues.

Stephanie and her friends made their way through the crowd into the lengthy, two-story chapel with long wooden pews and an arched ceiling. On their way to the front, they passed Rudy Cohen and Marsha Goodwin. Dressed in all black with a veiled hat, Marsha clung to Rudy's arm, sobbing. She looked up as they passed by, glaring at Stephanie with a hateful, accusing look.

No way am I going to give her the satisfaction of a response... she thought, looking away. She ignored the caustic diva and continued on.

The group solemnly made their way to the front where Jock's silver cremation urn sat on a table next to a large portrait of him. The table was surrounded by wall-to-wall flower arrangements. Stephanie looked for the wreath she had ordered—an open heart made with burgundy, pink, and a splash of white flowers. The banner across it read simply "Beloved," but the card attached to it contained a personal note from her. Someone had stuck the wreath behind a tall pedestal holding a vase of red roses.

Oh, well, she thought, assuming that the mortuary staff had arranged everything, *it's the thought that counts. Today isn't about me, anyway, it's about Jock.*

She stared at Jock's urn, finding it hard to fathom that the ashes inside were all that remained of him. This time last week they were having dinner at his favorite Italian restaurant. Now, sadly, he was nothing more than a memory. A deep sadness welled inside her. She reached into her purse for a tissue.

Jock's parents stood off to one side, receiving visitors and family members. Stephanie got in line to say a word to his mother, Patricia, but when it became her turn and she stood face-to-face with the woman, Patricia didn't appear to remember her.

"Jock introduced us at your nephew's wedding last spring," Stephanie said warmly. Jock got his height from his father, but his dark hair and deep brown eyes came from his mother.

Patricia looked confused. The overpowering scent of sandalwood perfume engulfed her like an ominous cloud. "You and Jock were friends?"

"We have been seeing each other for a year," Stephanie replied, wondering why Patricia was treating her like a complete stranger. When Jock introduced them, he'd made a point to inform his mother that she was his girlfriend.

"Well," Patricia said as she briefly squeezed Stephanie's hand, "thank you for coming." She abruptly turned away and began speaking to someone else.

Stunned, Stephanie stood like a statue, amazed at the woman's cool response. Fighting back tears of embarrassment and humiliation, she slowly pivoted to join her friends and found Valerie Hale watching her instead. The sympathetic look on Valerie's face indicated she had witnessed the encounter.

"Sorry about that, kid," Valerie said plainly. "She probably didn't mean to be rude. She's had a terrible week."

"I suppose she has," Stephanie replied, feeling guilty about bothering Patricia Tanner at a time like this. "How well do you know her?"

Valerie glanced at Patricia. "Our families are close. She's like a second mother to me."

Stephanie stepped aside so other people could get in line. "I'd better get out of the way. I need to find the people I came with anyway." She left Valerie and wandered through the chapel looking for Katie and the girls. The pews were already filling up for the service.

"Hey, there," someone said as she walked into the lobby. Curious, she turned around. It was Stuart Hale.

"Hi, Stu," Stephanie replied, relieved to find someone she knew. "If you're looking for Val, I just talked to her in the chapel."

Stuart Hale stood about six feet tall with salt and pepper hair, wearing a dark suit and blue striped shirt sans a tie. His grayish-green eyes scanned the emerald and diamond pendant hanging from her neck, then held her gaze. "She's the last person I want to run into right now. Funeral or not, she's hoping to corner me here so she can hit me up for money." He placed his hands on her shoulders. "I'm sorry about Jock. It's a heck of a way to lose someone. How are you holding up?"

"I'm fine," Stephanie said quickly, "but I need to ask you a question and I want the truth."

His eyes narrowed as though she'd caught him completely off guard. "Okay," he said warily. "What's on your mind?"

She glanced around to make sure no one was listening to their conversation then she leaned close. "Marsha Goodwin told me that she and Jock spent intimate weekends together in New York City. She claimed they were going to get married. Is that true?"

Stu responded with a wry laugh. "In her fantasies, maybe. It's true, Jock took her to New York with him a couple of times, but it was originally to fill the role of an assistant." He cleared his throat. "Things sort of got out of hand."

Now it was her turn to laugh. "Ya think?"

"He dumped her two weeks ago but she wouldn't accept it. I knew he regretted getting involved with her," Stu said seriously. "He always did when he cheated on you." Reaching up, Stu gently lifted her pendant with the tip of his finger. "Why do you think he showered you with such beautiful one-of-a-kind creations each time you found out and broke up with him? Penance, baby, penance," Stu let go of the necklace. "He loved you, Stephanie. You were the best thing that had ever happened to him. He wanted to marry *you*."

What? No way. True love doesn't cheat…

Her thoughts must have given away her shock and disbelief. "Trust me," he said quietly as he took her hands in his. "He loved you. I know he did."

Feeling completely unsettled by Stu's admission, she excused herself, saying she needed to locate her friends so they could find seats together in the chapel before the service started. "If you hurry," she told him, "you can sit with Val."

"No thanks. Besides, I can't stay." He shoved his hand into his pocket and pulled out his keys. "I'll see you later." He turned and wove through the crowd, making his way to the front entrance.

She watched him disappear, noticing something odd as he left the building. A man followed him out. An older man. The gentleman looked familiar, but she couldn't place him.

She found the girls sipping on glasses of ice water in the Friendship Room, a place where friends and family could gather and chat. "We'd better get going,' she said to Katie. "The chapel is already filling up."

People were still arriving as they maneuvered through the milling crowd, slowly making their way into the chapel. By the time they got there, it was nearly full. The only space available for them to sit together was in the very last row. Stephanie got the seat next to the aisle. She glanced at her phone. They still had fifteen minutes to go. Would it be rude to pass the time looking at her email? Everyone around her seemed to be looking at their phones.

She sensed a familiar presence and looked up. Shane stood in the aisle, waiting for people to find seats or keep moving along. The dip in his brows made him appear stressed.

"Shane," Stephanie called to him in a stage whisper. He looked her way, his expression changing from a troubled frown to instant relief as his gaze fell on her.

"Hi," he mouthed as he moved toward her. He bent down and whispered, "I wish I could stay here with you, but I'm expected to sit in the front row with the family." He held out a couple of sheets of paper. "Aunt Pat wrote the eulogy, but she wants me to give it in her place."

She sensed his nervousness. "You'll do fine."

He shook his head. "It would be different if she asked me to give it in front of the family at a private service, but the place is packed…"

She could totally relate to his discomfort.

"I've found a way to make public speaking easy," she whispered, hoping to give him some encouragement and put him at ease. "Do what I've learned to do when I have to speak in front of a crowd at the store's fashion shows. Keep your finger on the text and move it along as you're reading so you don't lose your place. Don't look up for more than a second at a time or you'll get distracted. Just keep going at an even pace and concentrate solely on the speech until you're done. Then say thank you, and leave the podium."

He flashed a grateful smile. "Thanks. I'll try that."

By the time the service started, people had lined the back wall and filled the reception area. Stephanie looked toward the front to find Shane and saw Valerie sitting next to Patricia Tanner. Patricia had her arm around Valerie, as though she was Jock's girlfriend.

It doesn't matter. I'm beyond the hurt of being overlooked, Stephanie thought as she stared down at her clasped hands. *I've paid my respects to Jock tonight. I'm moving on.*

Katie squeezed Stephanie's hand and leaned close. "You should investigate Jock's murder."

Stephanie blinked in amazement. "What?"

"I saw on the news that the police don't have any idea who killed him and they're asking for the public's help, but you could find out who did it," Katie whispered.

"Me?" Stephanie pointed toward herself. "Why me?"

Katie raised her brows above her black-framed glasses. "Why not you?"

Stephanie uttered a wry chuckle under her breath. "I have no expertise in that area. I'm not an officer of the law."

"Exactly," Katie countered. "People will feel free to talk to you. They'll tell you things they won't tell the cops."

Right, Stephanie thought cynically. *No way would someone like Marsha Goodwin or Rudy Cohen confess anything to ME.* She opened her mouth to argue with Katie about it when someone in the row ahead turned and silenced her with a loud, "S-h-h-h!"

She cleared her throat, dropped her gaze to the floor, and

remained silent after that.

The service began at seven sharp and lasted about an hour. Once it was over, everyone stood at once and crowded together, silently advancing through the building toward the entrance like a slow-moving stream of zombies. Stephanie breathed a sigh of relief when they finally exited the building into the crisp evening air. "The mood in there was so dreary," she announced as she drew in a deep breath. "I could barely breathe."

Nora pulled out her keys. "Anyone want to stop for coffee and dessert?"

"Not me," Katie replied looking at her watch. "It's after eight o'clock and I need to take Stephanie home. I have to work tomorrow."

"I'll take her home," Shane's voice boomed over the top of Stephanie's head. He whispered into her ear, "I need to get out of here."

Chapter Seven

Stephanie waved goodbye to her friends as Shane led her to Jock's Navigator.

"I told my aunt you needed a ride home. I hope you don't mind that I used you as an excuse to ditch my family. I had to leave," he said sounding desperate. "The atmosphere was so depressing and stuffy in that place I thought I was going to suffocate."

"That's what I thought, too!" Stephanie cried as he opened the passenger door and took her hand, guiding her into the vehicle.

"Jock hated funerals. I'm sure he wouldn't have wanted all of this fuss, but it wasn't up to him." Shane shut her door and trotted around to the driver's side. "I'm hungry," he said as he slid in and shoved his key into the ignition. "I never got a chance to eat dinner. Do you want to stop somewhere and have a pizza?"

The day had been long and the memorial service, draining. The thought of going to a busy restaurant with loud music and lots of people sounded exhausting. She just wanted to go home and get into her jammies. "Why don't we eat it at my house? I'll order one to be delivered."

"Sounds good to me." He pulled out of the chapel parking lot and stepped on the gas as if he couldn't get away fast enough.

She drew her phone from her purse and searched for the number of her favorite pizzeria. She was still full from dinner but figured since he was giving her a ride home, she could be cordial and eat one slice. He sounded like he was hungry enough to eat most of it anyway.

"They're running behind tonight," she said after she placed her food order. "We should make it to my place in plenty of time before the pizza arrives." She grabbed her purse and tossed her phone into it. "By the way, your eulogy was great."

He gave her an appreciative smile. "I took your advice. When I looked up, I focused on you."

"I noticed that."

Their gazes locked briefly, but long enough to convey that he'd focused on her for more reasons than the one he just gave.

"I ran into Stuart Hale at the service," she said, changing the subject. "I asked him about Jock and Marsha. Stu told me that Jock *was* shacking up with her on the weekends he went to New York City, *but* just before he was murdered, he dumped her. Hmph…" She rolled her eyes. "Why does that not surprise me? The thing is, she lied to me about Jock wanting to marry her. I wonder what else she's lied about to me— and to Detective Garrett."

"Obviously, showing her the door wasn't what she was expecting him to do," Shane replied seriously. "I'm no detective, but I'd say it's a motive for murder."

Stephanie crossed her arms and nodded in agreement. "Yep."

She instructed Shane to pull into the alley and park next to the garage. They opened the gate and walked through the backyard, entering the house by the back porch. They both saw the screen sitting on the floor next to the open window at the same time.

"Wait here," Shane said in a warning voice. He opened the back door—which was unlocked now—and cautiously entered the dark kitchen. He found the light switch and flipped it on, flooding the room with bright light.

Stephanie peered through the window as she waited for him to check out the house and wondered why Hobbit wasn't barking. Shane's presence should have set him off. She began to worry that something bad had happened to him.

Shane looked through the small house and turned on all of the lights as he went. "You can come in now," he said as he returned to the kitchen. "Whoever was here is gone."

Stephanie shot through the door. "Where is Hobbit?"

Shane pointed toward the downstairs bedroom. "Curled up in his bed. He looked up at me when I turned on the light, but then he went right back to sleep."

"That's not like h—" She finished the sentence with a gasp. Her living room had been literally turned inside out. The contents of the closet and bookcase lay strewn across the floor. Every picture had been removed from the walls; every drawer had been dumped out. Someone had even upended the living room furniture. "Oh, my gosh..." she screeched. "What happened to my house?"

"I'm sorry," Shane said gravely. "I don't understand why someone would do this, but it's obvious they were desperate to find something."

Stunned, Stephanie stepped over the debris as she made her way into the bedroom.

Hobbit lay curled up in his bed, sleeping like a baby. She knelt to examine him. "How are you doing, buddy? Are you okay?" He licked her hand and yawned, but didn't attempt to get up. Why was he so sleepy?

Shane stepped over the contents of a dresser drawer. "I know you're upset, but as far as you can tell, is there anything missing?"

She stood with her hands on her hips, fighting back tears as she looked around. "Gosh, I won't know until I clean up this mess."

Her dresser drawers had been dumped on the bed—the contents cast about as though someone had riffled through them. Her jewelry case stood open and some of her jewelry had fallen out, laying in a tangled heap on the floor. The contents of her closet had been torn apart as well. Purses, shoes—everything on the top shelf was now a heap of spilled boxes on the floor. She swallowed hard. "I can't believe this..."

Shane stared at her jewelry case. "I find it hard to believe that someone would break into your house and not steal your jewelry. What were they looking for?"

Their gazes locked. "The diamonds," they said at the same time.

"Someone isn't convinced that I'm innocent," Stephanie complained, angry at the condition of her house. She and Shane went back into the kitchen, stepping carefully around the items on the floor along the way. "Well, I hope they're happy now. They didn't find any diamonds but they had fun destroying my home while I was at a funeral."

Shane turned around. "It couldn't have been anyone we know. They were all in the chapel."

"That's right... Oh, wait a minute," Stephanie said as she grabbed her purse. "Stu left before the service started."

Shane stared at her in surprise. "Are you sure?"

"Yeah. He told me he was leaving. I saw him go." She opened her purse and rummaged through it, looking for Detective Garrett's card.

Shane glanced out of the window, staring at Evelyn Bona's house. "We should pay a visit to your neighbor. Maybe she saw someone around the yard at the time of the break-in. If it was Stu, perhaps she could describe him."

"Evelyn?" Stephanie frowned as she dialed her phone. "She's gone on Wednesday nights. She meets her pals for a potluck dinner at the senior center then they all play bridge." She put the phone to her ear, waiting for Detective Garrett to answer. "Believe me, if Evelyn saw anything she would have called the police immediately and then called me. Then she would have called my mother!" Stephanie didn't plan to tell Vera anything about the break-in until she had more information. She didn't want to worry her parents. Or get them upset.

To her disappointment, she got the detective's voicemail. She left a message and hoped he'd call her back right away.

She set her phone on the counter next to an empty dog food can. A large one. "This is why the dog is sleeping so soundly." She picked it up, showing it to Shane. "He's full to the gills! This is a lot more than he gets in an entire day. I'm surprised he hasn't thrown it all up. Someone must have fed him all of that food to keep him busy while they ransacked the house."

Her phone rang. It was Inga. "Hi, Inga," Stephanie said. "How are you doing?"

"I'm fine," Inga's light, feminine voice replied. "I'm calling to see how *you're* doing. You looked pretty sad throughout the service. Are you okay?"

"Well," Stephanie countered with a sigh, "I was okay until I got home." She paused. "Someone broke into my house while I was gone."

Inga gasped. "Oh, no. That's terrible! What did they steal?"

"So far," Stephanie glanced around, "I can't see that they took anything. I mean, my TV and my jewelry are still here, but the place has been ransacked."

"Did you call 9-1-1?"

"I called the detective who is investigating Jock's murder," Stephanie replied. "I think whoever broke in was looking for the diamonds that Jock has supposedly embezzled from the store."

"Did you call your parents? What did they say?"

The doorbell rang. "That's the pizza," Stephanie said, glad for an excuse to get off the line. "I have to go, but thanks for calling to check on me, Inga. I'm okay—really. I'll talk to you tomorrow. Bye."

Shane pulled his wallet from his pocket as he walked to the door. "I'll get this." He paid the driver, grabbed the box, and shut the door. The room filled with the spicy aroma of freshly baked sausage pizza with extra cheese.

Stephanie stared at the carnage surrounding her, getting anxious to dig in and put everything back in its rightful place. "I need to get this mess cleaned up. It's going to take hours."

Shane set the pizza box on the table. "You'd better leave everything as it is until Garrett gets here. He'll need to see what happened and get pictures of the scene." He opened the box. "C'mon. We might as well eat while we wait for him to call back."

"Okay," Stephanie said, knowing he was right. For now, she couldn't do anything until the detective arrived and examined the scene. She opened the refrigerator. "I'll grab a couple of cans of Coke." On her way back to the table with the Cokes, she also picked up two plates and grabbed a roll of paper towels.

Shane sat down and pulled several large slices of pizza from the box. "I think you should stay with your parents tonight. You're not safe here."

"I don't see why." Stephanie grabbed the pull tab on her Coke can and popped it open with a loud 'snap!' A bubbly sheen of effervescence shot through the opening. "Whoever broke in tonight knows now that I don't have the diamonds so they will look elsewhere."

Shane gave her a dubious look. "Maybe…" He ate a large bite of his pizza. "What if he's not convinced? What if he's concluded you're storing them somewhere else?" He shook his head. "You're taking a chance. He might come back when you're home and confront you."

"I'll make sure all the windows and doors are locked before I go to bed." She tore off a couple of sheets of paper towels and handed him a section. "I can't live my life in fear. Besides, staying somewhere else will make it look like I have something to hide."

Shane didn't argue with her, but his deep frown indicated he didn't approve.

They were cleaning up the pizza dishes when the doorbell rang. Hobbit scrambled out of the bedroom and barked at the noise. Oh, sure. Now he was concerned about strangers!

Detective Garrett stood on the front stoop. "I got your message. Did you call 911?"

Stephanie shook her head and stood aside to let him in, ignoring the dog's growls and snorts of disapproval. "You told me to call *you* if I had any other information. Here it is." She made a wide sweep of her hand to show him the damage. "This isn't an ordinary burglary. Whoever broke into my house must think I'm hiding the diamonds." She looked up as he entered the living room. "As far as I can tell, they didn't take anything. They didn't even take my jewelry."

Detective Garrett wore a poker face, taking in every detail as he walked through the house, examining the scene and asking questions. They showed him the unlocked window where the intruder had gotten in. He promptly advised Stephanie to install an alarm system.

After they left, Shane replaced the screen on the back window and then locked the window and the back door. Then he went through the house, checking every window to make sure they were locked tight.

"Do you need help putting everything away?" he asked as he

turned her sofa upright and walked around the room, setting the furniture back into place.

"I think it would go faster if I did it myself because I know where everything goes," she replied, "but thanks for the offer."

"No problem." He sounded disappointed. "I'll lock the door as I leave." He pulled his vehicle key from his pocket and walked to the front entrance. He stopped and turned back, hesitating as though he wanted to say something else. "I'll call you tomorrow."

Shane pulled open the door and took a step backward.

Inga and Katie stood on the stoop, wide-eyed with surprise. Katie's finger rested on the doorbell, but when she saw him, she pulled it back.

Stephanie stepped out from behind Shane. "Hey, what are you guys doing here so late? Don't you have to work tomorrow?"

"We're worried about you so we've decided to stay with you tonight," Katie announced as she pushed past Shane. Inga trooped in behind her. "Okay?"

Stephanie knew better than to argue with *them*.

Chapter Eight

The next afternoon, Stephanie clocked out at the boutique at four o'clock and headed home. "Goodnight," she said airily to June, the owner, and pushed open the front door. "See you tomorrow."

The cloudy, mid-September afternoon had a slight breeze, making the cool, damp air even more chilly. She stopped and slipped her fawn-colored, cashmere poncho over her peach dress. In the process, her sunglasses fell from her purse. She bent down to pick them up and when she looked up, she noticed a man at the sidewalk café across the street, sitting at a small table. He appeared to be drinking coffee and casually reading the paper. On any other day, she wouldn't have thought twice about it, but something about him gave her pause. Besides it being a lousy day to sit outside, he looked vaguely familiar, though she couldn't place where she'd seen him before.

But then, suddenly…she remembered.

Shoving her sunglasses into her purse, she walked swiftly down the street to catch her bus which was due any moment. At the bus stop, she took a seat inside the long, but narrow glassed-in transit shelter and glanced through the clear-paned wall.

The man was gone…

She pulled the soft, warm poncho tighter around her, shivering from the creeped-out feeling his presence—and disappearance had given her.

The bus pulled up and she sprang from her seat, bounding across the sidewalk and into the vehicle. She swiped her metro bus card across the card reader and took an open seat. As soon as the vehicle pulled away from the transit shelter, she dug her phone out of her purse and dialed Shane.

"Hey," Shane said, sounding happy. Soft music from a local radio station echoed through the phone, indicating he was in the SUV. "I was just about to give you a call. How about dinner tonight? I'll pick you up from work."

"You'll have to meet me at home. I'm on the bus right now," Stephanie said. "I have to let my dog out or he'll pee on the rug by the back door."

"There's an Irish pub downtown on the Nicollet Mall," he said quickly. "I haven't been to that place in a long time, but the last time I ate there with Jock, they had great food."

"I know the one," she said, deciding to wait until they were together to tell him about the man at the cafe. "I'll be home in twenty minutes."

"Sounds good," he said. "I've got something I need to show you."

Really? she thought. *I wonder what that could be.*

"Okay," she said and stared out the window, watching buildings go by as the bus rambled along Lyndale Avenue. "I've got something I need to discuss with you too. See you then."

*   *   *

Stephanie arrived home to find Jock's black Navigator parked at the curb. Wearing a purple Minnesota Vikings hoodie over a gold t-shirt and jeans, Shane slid out of the vehicle and met her on the sidewalk in front of her house. "Hey," he said, his eyes twinkling. The bold scent of his cologne surrounded him like an invisible cloak. "You look terrific."

"Thanks," she replied, "but I'm freezing in this dress. I've got to find something warmer and more comfortable to wear to the pub." She shivered as she pulled her keys from her purse and hustled toward the front door. "Let's hurry. I need to get out of this wind."

"Let me go in first," he announced, taking on a serious tone. "I want to make sure the person who broke in last night didn't come back to take another look around." He followed her and pushed open the door as soon as she unlocked it, brushing past her.

Hobbit raced around the living room, barking up a storm.

Shane walked from room to room as Stephanie waited inside the entry. "Everything looks fine," he said, coming back into the living room. "You did fast work cleaning up the mess."

Stephanie laughed. "Katie and Inga were a great help. It was so late they were motivated to work fast. Each of us took a room and got the house put back in order in a little over an hour." She dumped her purse on the dining room table and walked into the kitchen, turning on the lights as she went. Hobbit raced her to the back door. She let him outdoors to do his business. "Help yourself to a Coke," she said to Shane as she went into her bedroom to change clothes. She shut the bedroom door, kicked off her heels, stepped out of her dress, and slid into a pair of black corduroy leggings and a pink Vera Wang sweater.

Feeling refreshed, she returned to the kitchen and took a can of dog food from the pantry. She popped the top and dropped a tablespoon of food into Hobbit's dish. "I'll be right back." She went out to the back porch to let the dog back into the house.

Hobbit raced into the kitchen with Stephanie following behind as he made a beeline for his dish. She smiled at Shane. "Our evening ritual. He waits for me to come home every night."

Hobbit ignored them, gobbling his food.

Stephanie grabbed a Coke from the refrigerator and sat across from Shane at the dining room table. "What did you want to talk to me about?"

He zipped open his hoodie and pulled a sheath of vertically folded papers from the waistband of his jeans. "I found this today while I was cleaning out the Lincoln." He placed the papers on the table and pushed them toward her. "I think this is what Jock wanted to discuss with me the day we were supposed to meet at the James J. Hill festival."

"What is it?" Her breath caught in her throat as she picked up the papers and unfolded them.

"It's a partial copy of his will."

"His will?" She stared at the first printed page, marked with crossed-out words, arrows, and scribbled phrases in Jock's scrawling handwriting. "But the police searched his vehicle. Why didn't they find it?"

"It got caught between the seat and the console," Shane said. "The only reason I found it was because some change fell out of my pocket while I was paying for my burgers at a drive-through. When I shoved my fingers down there to get the coins, I cut my finger on the edge of one of the pages."

It took a few moments for the words on the document to register in her brain, but once she realized what the penned-in remarks indicated, she stared at it in disbelief. "Oh, my gosh…"

"Yeah." Shane nodded. "It looks like he had planned to change his will and make you the beneficiary of everything."

She swallowed hard and blinked back tears, stunned at the revised content of the document. "I leave my entire estate to my dearest *wife*, Stephanie…" She read the words aloud slowly, trying to make sense of it all. Stu was right. Jock was planning to ask her to marry him. His actions appeared to be sincere, but…would it have lasted? Would he have truly turned over a new leaf and become faithful to her, or would time have faded the luster of his good intentions?

"I guess now we know why he broke things off with Marsha," Shane said, seemingly reading her thoughts. "He planned to propose to you and changing his will indicates to me that he expected to get married right away."

He sounded sad—or was that a thread of skepticism in his reply?

"Jock had a jewelry convention in Las Vegas next month at the Bellagio and he wanted me to go with him. He probably planned to surprise me with his proposal and get married the same weekend," she said quietly. "Just the two of us. Jock didn't like fanfare." She let out a deep breath and looked away. "At the service last night, Stu told me that Jock wanted to marry me, but I didn't believe him." She reached into her purse and pulled out a tissue. "I thought once the memorial service was over, I'd stop crying about Jock and get on with my life, but I guess he just won't let me go." She sniffled and wiped her nose with the tissue. "He was probably designing a beautiful wedding set for me." She wasn't in love with him any longer but realizing how he must have felt about her made her sad. Could their marriage have survived? Knowing Jock, it was doubtful.

Shane took a swig of his Coke. "I hate to say this, but if Jock left it in the safe at the store, you'll never get it out of Rudy. If you confront him, he'll most likely deny it."

"You're probably right." She thought about how Jock's mother had hurt her feelings when the woman refused to acknowledge her at the memorial service. She pushed the thought from her mind, determined to let it go. "It makes me sad to think Rudy would be that vindictive, but maybe it's for the best. This last year with Jock has been crazy. I need to put everything connected with him and his family behind me and get on with my life."

They sat in silence for a little while, drinking their Cokes. Gazing through the dining room window, she watched as Evelyn exited the back door of her house wearing a thick blue sweater and carrying a brown grocery bag filled with newspapers. She lifted the lid of her recycling bin and dropped it inside.

Stephanie froze. The newspapers reminded her of the incident at work…

She gasped.

Shane looked up. "What?"

"I think I'm being followed."

He sat rigid, his eyes widening. "When? Where? Tell me what happened."

"I think someone has been tailing me since the day Jock was murdered," Stephanie began. "When I met my friends at the bookstore on Friday night, I saw a man looking at a magazine. I didn't realize it at the time, but he was watching me. I saw him again at the service last night. He left right after Stu did. Then today, he was sitting at the café across the street when I left work. He pretended to be reading a newspaper, but I think he was waiting for me to leave the building so he could follow me."

Shane's eyes narrowed. "What did he look like?"

"Older with white hair and wire-rimmed glasses," Stephanie said. "He always wears khaki slacks and a brown bill cap. I didn't put it all together until today when I saw him sitting at the café."

"So, he followed Stu out of the funeral home…" Shane rubbed his chin, deep in thought. "I wonder if they're working together."

She sipped her Coke. "Maybe this man was Jock's silent partner and he's looking for the diamonds, too."

"I know you don't want to get involved in solving Jock's murder or finding the diamonds," Shane said gravely, "but I think you're already in deeper than you realize. Too many issues are coming to light to ignore."

"You're right, I don't want to get involved," she replied with a sigh. "But after what happened last night, it's clear that I don't have any choice in the matter."

Shane looked around. "We need a pen and paper. We have to make a list of everyone we know and their motives for wanting Jock dead."

Stephanie rose and went to the built-in bureau lining one wall of the dining room. She pulled out a drawer and grabbed a wire-bound notebook. "I've got a pen in my purse." She dropped it on the table and sat down then grabbed her bag and dug around in it, searching for one but all she could come up with was a long plastic box. "I must have left my last pen at work. We're always short because customers accidentally take them. I guess I'll have to use this one." She opened the box and took out the pen Jock had given her.

"Whoa," Shane said, his mouth gaping at the diamond-studded fountain pen. "Where did you get that?"

"Jock gave it to me as a peace offering the last time we got back together," she said as she twirled the heavy pen between her fingers. "It's called *The Marilyn* because, you know, diamonds are a girl's best friend. Jock said it contains over nineteen hundred diamonds. The barrel is platinum and the nib," she pointed to the sharp tip where the ink flowed through, "is eighteen-carat gold. He told me it was worth a lot of money, so I promised to protect it and not show it to anyone. He said it would make a good investment for me in case anything ever happened to him—" She swallowed at the irony of that statement. "Because diamonds never go down in value, they only increase."

Shane whistled in amazement and held out his palm. "May I look at it?"

"Sure." She handed it to him. "It's so heavy, I can barely write with it. I've been carrying it in my purse to keep it safe. After what happened last night, I'm glad I did." She pointed to the diamonds crowning the pen. "Look how it sparkles in the light. Do you think this is what the thief was looking for?"

He shook his head. "According to Stu, Rudy is missing millions of dollars. *Millions...*" He stared at her. "The stash is sitting in a safe place somewhere, but the problem is...where?"

Shane handed the pen back to her and she opened her notebook to a blank page. "Okay, so let's start." She drew a line down the center, making two columns, then wrote a name in the first column. "I'd say Rudy has the greatest motive for killing Jock. He stands to gain twice. First, the diamonds are probably insured for theft or embezzlement, so he'll get his money back if they aren't found. And second, he'll collect Jock's life insurance policy, which is worth millions, too." She wrote "insurance claims" in the second column.

"Marsha was jilted, losing her lover and a potential rich husband," Shane added. "That makes her number two in my book."

"Stuart Hale was one of Jock's closest friends—and his accountant," Stephanie chimed in. "He may have known about everything except where Jock hid the diamonds. He's always strapped for money because Val goes through her alimony check like water through a sieve then she cooks up one scheme after another to get more out of him." She wrote both names in the book and their respective motives.

Shane drummed his fingers on the table. "Maybe he was Jock's partner…"

"What about the guy following me?" Stephanie wrote "stranger" in the name column and set the heavy pen down. The sheer weight of it was beginning to make her hand tired. "He could have been Jock's partner, or Stu's. Maybe he's working for Rudy!"

"Yeah," Shane said sounding dubious. "That's the problem. We don't know who he is or what his motive is." He pointed to the list. "You'd better just put a question mark in the motive column until we find out more about him."

How will we do that? she wondered. "Okay," she said slowly. The thought of chasing down this guy to find out who he was and why he was following her gave her the chills. She didn't want to get involved, but ever since the break-in, she'd known in her heart that she could no longer look the other way. Someone believed she had those diamonds and was determined to find them. Would he kill her to get his hands on them? She remembered the gypsy's warning and shivered.

Your life is in danger, watch out for the stranger;

dark days ahead are dawning..."

Chapter Nine

Stephanie and Shane made one more list before they left for the pub. They wrote down every place they could think of where Jock might have hidden information leading them to the diamonds. Together, they concluded there must be a considerable number of stones to be valued in the millions and that Jock would not have stored them anywhere that made them easily discovered.

But where were they? Sitting somewhere in a safety deposit box? If so, wouldn't Stu have known about it?

"I'll drop you off here and park in the ramp around the corner," Shane said as he pulled up to the front door of the pub. "If you get seated before I get back, order a Guinness for me."

Stephanie walked into the pub and found it crowded with wall-to-wall revelers enjoying lively conversation over their drinks and the toe-tapping music of an Irish folk tune. She loved this place with its high ceilings, tiled floors, dark wood, and a mural of an Irish warrior princess above the solid oak bar. She had to wait for a couple of minutes to be seated, but it was worth the hassle to get a "snug" — a wood-and-glass-enclosed booth with a view of the street.

As soon as her server arrived at her table, she ordered a Guinness for

Shane and a Coke for herself. When the server returned with the beverages, she ordered an appetizer of "pub pretzels" with dipping sauce.

Someone tapped on the window. She glanced up from perusing the dinner menu to find Shane on the sidewalk in front of the building waving at her. Moments later, he slid into the booth. His wind-tousled hair fell in unruly blond curls across his forehead.

"Nice table," he said happily and picked up his glass of Guinness, a dark, ruby-red ale. He took a healthy swig and sighed. "Ah, that hits the spot." He gazed into her eyes. "What's the dinner special tonight?"

"I don't know," Stephanie replied, puzzled. "I think it was written on a chalkboard by the entrance, but I didn't pay much attention to it when I walked in." She laughed. "I always look over the menu, but I end up eating the same thing every time I come here."

They sat in silence for a few minutes studying the menu, but Shane kept drumming one finger on the table, as though his mind was somewhere else.

She pushed her menu away, bored with looking at the dessert section.

The server appeared with their warm pretzels and two small dishes of dipping sauce. They placed their dinner order—two plates of Irish fish and chips—then started munching on the pretzels.

Stephanie dipped a pretzel into a dish of cheese sauce and nibbled on it as she studied him. "When are you going back to California?"

He picked up a pretzel and dipped it into the dish containing a spicy sauce. "Not for a couple more weeks at least. My next film is on hold until Dack finishes physical therapy on his shoulder. If that doesn't work, he might need surgery." He shook his head in disapproval. "Dack flipped his Mercedes last month driving through Big Sur in the fog. I heard he had been drinking and was driving too fast. He was lucky he didn't sustain worse injuries. He totaled the car." Shane looked up. "In any case, the delay gives me more time to work with Jock's parents and his attorney on settling his estate." He sighed. "Unfortunately, it's going to take a lot longer than a few weeks…"

Jock's murder and Rudy's embezzlement claim aren't helping matters either, Stephanie thought as she sipped her Coke. What a mess. Perhaps it was a blessing that Jock's family wouldn't acknowledge her relationship with him. It kept her out of the current family crisis as well.

Shane suddenly reached across the table and grabbed her hand. The firm grip of his long fingers encasing hers made her heart flutter. "Let's not talk about our problems anymore tonight. Okay? We came here to have fun." He held up his beer glass. "Cheers!"

Stephanie raised her glass and touched the rim against his. "Cheers!"

Still, the problem of who had ransacked her house lurked in the back of her mind, clouding her joy.

* * *

Since tomorrow was a workday, Shane brought Stephanie home from the pub at around eight o'clock. He parked the SUV in front of the house and even though the building was locked up tight, he insisted on walking through the rooms before Stephanie entered.

"Just to be safe," he said as he waited for her to unlock the front door, "stay in the entry like you did last time until I tell you it's okay to come in."

Stephanie sighed with impatience but did what he asked as he went through the house, switching on the light in every room. Why would the intruder come back? He didn't find what he was looking for so he was probably looking somewhere else—ransacking some other unsuspecting person's house.

Hobbit followed Shane from room to room, barking with excitement and wiggling his tail so hard it made his back-half dance from side to side. The dog had become used to Shane's presence and started welcoming him whenever he came around.

"Everything looks fine," Shane said, returning to the entryway.

"Good." Stephanie rounded the divider into the living room and dropped her purse on the coffee table. "Hobbit needs to go outside."

And put his signature on the corner of the house... she thought wryly.

Shane unlocked the kitchen door and led the way through the back porch. He opened the screen door and Hobbit rushed past him into the night, eager to take care of his business.

Stephanie flipped the switch to turn on the outdoor light, but it wouldn't go on. She'd forgotten the bulb had burned out—a month ago—and she had been procrastinating changing it because it was too high to reach without a stepladder. She had put off the task of getting the stepladder from the garage, dragging it across the lawn, and climbing on it to change the light because...what a pain.

She shrugged and followed him out into the chilly evening air under a cloudy sky. The breeze had stilled and the only sounds in the neighborhood were the singsong hum of a few crickets and the steady rumble of a neighbor's electric garage door rolling down. Evelyn's house looked dark except for a small light in the hallway, indicating she'd gone out for the evening.

Hobbit sniffed at his favorite corner of the house but kept on going into the backyard.

"What the heck…" Her eyes hadn't adjusted to the dark yet, but thanks to the silvery light cast by the streetlight at the end of the alley, her gaze could follow the dark figure of her dog crossing the yard. He stopped at several mounds in the corner where her roses grew. What was that? Her shoe tops were quickly covered with dew as her feet swished through the wet grass. The closer she got, the more suspicious she became…

She suddenly tripped over something. Pitching forward, she stumbled and fell into a pile of dirt. Thankfully, falling on her palms saved her from landing face-first on the ground. Getting her bearings, she stood up, smacking the soil off her dew-covered hands as her eyes focused, taking in the mounds of dirt and upended root balls scattered about. Gingerly, she stuck out her foot to see what had tripped her, tapping her shoe against the handle of a shovel. Someone had dug up her garden!

"My roses…" Placing her hands over her heart, she gasped in horror. "Look what someone did to my roses!" She picked up the shovel and turned to Shane who stood on the sidewalk in front of the porch steps. "Why would someone do this to me?"

He walked toward her. "I don't know, but my guess is that whoever did this was looking to see if you'd buried the diamonds under the bushes." He stopped in front of her and let out a tense sigh. "It was probably the same person who broke into your house."

The very idea made her jaw clench with ire. Breaking into her house was stressful enough, but destroying her beautiful, expensive plants crossed a line that set her off on a tantrum of biblical proportions. She'd spent the last two years caring for these pricey rosebushes, coaxing huge, beautiful blooms out of them—only to have this happen? Who was responsible for this senseless act of mean-spirited vandalism?

She threw down the shovel and stamped her foot with each shouted word. "This…is…*it!* The last straw! I am so done with this missing diamond business. So *done*!" She stomped past the flowerbed with clenched fists, kicking the shovel out of her way. "If I ever get my hands on the person who did this, he's going to wish he had never messed with me!"

Shane squinted in the dark, surveying the damage. "I'm no expert, but as far as I can tell, he didn't get all of them." He picked up the shovel. "We must have interrupted him when we arrived." He scratched his head, obviously at a loss as to what to do next. "The bushes can be replanted, right? Maybe we can get a light out here and put them back in the ground." He looked up. "Do you think that would work?"

"Yeah, we can do that," Stephanie said, distracted. "We'll have to replace the bulb in the porch light first. I have a yard light on the garage, too, that can be angled toward the backyard. That should give us enough light to make temporary repairs."

"What's going on out here?" Valerie appeared on her back step in a fluffy red bathrobe, her hair wrapped in a thick towel. The bright lights from her kitchen illuminated her face. "Why are you shrieking?"

Stephanie spun around. "Did you notice anyone lurking around the alley or in my yard tonight, Val?"

Valerie shook her head. "I've been on my treadmill and listening to an audiobook. I just got out of the shower. What happened?"

Stephanie winced at the carnage. "Someone dug up my flowers. We think he was looking for Jock's diamonds."

Valerie gasped. "Stephanie, are you serious?"

Stephanie shrugged. "I can't think of any other reason why anyone would waste their time tearing up my backyard!"

Valerie gripped the handle of her glass storm door and pulled it open. "Why don't you check with Evelyn? She probably had her nose to the window as usual. She must have seen whoever did it."

Stephanie shook her head. "Evelyn isn't home tonight. She's probably babysitting her grandkids. That's the only time she stays out this late."

Valerie reached up with her free hand and pulled her lapels together to keep her neck warm. "Can you replant them?"

"Yes..." Stephanie placed her hands on her hips. "I'm going to put them back into the ground right away. I think they'll survive."

Valerie shivered. "I'm cold. I've got to get back inside." She opened the door. "Good luck. I hope you find the culprit."

"Thanks." Stephanie waved as Valerie disappeared into her house. She turned to Shane. "I'll get my keys and turn on the garage light. Do me a favor and change the bulb in the porch light, will you? I'll get you a replacement." She let out a loud sigh. "Boy, what a night this has turned out to be."

"I'm sorry, Stephanie," he said softly. "We'll get your garden replanted, but then I think we need to get serious about looking for clues as to who is doing this." He suddenly pulled her close, wrapping his arms around her. "Whoever is doing this seems to be convinced that the diamonds are hidden somewhere on your property. There is nothing to stop them from coming back again. I'm worried about you."

The warmth of his broad chest was comforting against her palms. The grip of his arms holding her close told her how much he cared about their friendship and it gave her a warm feeling inside. Without hesitation, she slipped her arms around his waist and sighed, knowing she couldn't stay on the sidelines any longer. "I'll call Detective Garrett and let him know what happened, but I won't mention that we're going to investigate this creep ourselves," she said as she pressed her cheek against his chest. "He wouldn't approve, but since it's clear he's not making any progress, we need to do something." She looked up. "When do we start?"

"We already have," Shane replied emphatically. "Tomorrow we'll go to the first location on our list and turn the place over. One way or another, we're going to find out who is doing this and stop this guy."

It sounded like a good plan, but...

Could two amateur sleuths actually catch the culprit and turn him over to the police? Only time would tell.

Chapter Ten

The next morning, Stephanie left the house to catch the bus when she noticed Jock's SUV parked at the curb. Shane sat motionless behind the wheel. Was he waiting for her to give her a ride to work? If so, why hadn't he called her to let her know he was out there or simply knocked on the front door?

She walked over to the SUV and peered through the passenger side window. He was sleeping! Had he been there all night? If so, why?

She went back into the house, nuked a leftover cup of coffee, and marched back out the front door to wake him up. When she reached the vehicle, he jerked awake, looking around in blurry-eyed confusion at the tap-tap-tap of her knuckles on the window.

"Good morning," she announced with curiosity as the glass silently slid down and disappeared into the door. She stepped on the running board and reached into the vehicle, offering him the mug of coffee. "Here—you look like you could use this."

His eyes widened at the mist curling from the large, flat-bottomed mug. The rich aroma of French roast filled the car. "Thanks. Boy, does that smell good." He accepted the mug and sat back, sipping the hot liquid as she walked around to the other side, opened the passenger door, and slid in.

"What are you doing here?" She dropped her purse on the floor and shut the door. "Have you been here all night?"

He merely grunted his answer, preoccupied with blowing on his coffee to cool it down.

Hmmm... she thought wryly. *We're not being very helpful. Are we grouchy, too?*

She turned toward him, twisting at the waist. "Why did you sleep in the car? Are you on the outs with your parents or something?"

He shook his head. The reddish tinge of a day's growth on his jaw proved he hadn't been home, but it only added to his rugged image of a Hollywood stuntman. "I was worried about you, Stephanie. I couldn't go home and leave you here alone." His golden brows furrowed. "What if the thief came back and broke into your house while you were sleeping?"

She smiled inwardly. In a way, that was so sweet of him to be concerned about her, but the reality was, if the intruder came through the back way again, Shane would never have known about it. The guy would never get past the deadbolt on her front door and all of her windows were locked, so he would obviously try the back door again. It was old and the lock was much easier to jimmy. Her dad had been meaning to install a deadbolt in that one too but hadn't gotten around to it yet.

"Why would he want to," she replied quizzically. "He didn't find anything the first time he broke in and he certainly didn't find anything by digging up my yard." She sighed in irritation. "That reminds me, I have a huge mess back there to clean up when I get home tonight."

Shane set his cup on the console. "I'll help you with that," he offered sincerely, "after we get back from Majestic Jewelers."

She tensed at the thought of confronting Marsha again. "I hope they don't throw us out when they realize what we're up to." She rolled her eyes. "Both Rudy and Marsha suspect me of hoarding the diamonds and when I show up at the store, they'll probably think I'm nosing around to make sure Jock didn't leave any evidence pointing to me as his co-conspirator."

Shane tiredly ran his hand through his thick, wavy hair, as he let out a huge yawn. "Frankly, I don't care what they think. As the executor of Jock's will, I have a perfect right to enter the premises to look through his office. If you happen to be with me, so be it."

Stephanie checked her watch. "Okay, well, I'd better get going or I'll miss the next bus and I'll be late getting to work."

He started the car. "I'll give you a ride. I'm on my way home anyway to take a hot shower and hit the sack for a few hours." He turned on the vehicle's blinker and glanced over his shoulder for oncoming traffic. "What time do you get off? I'll pick you up."

"Thankfully, I've got a short shift today," she said, grabbing his mug to keep it from spilling. "I really don't feel like working. I'm off at two."

"Great." He nodded. "I'll be there at two sharp. Call me right away if you see that old guy hanging around outside the store."

She let out a deep breath. "Okay." The last thing she wanted to do today was to encounter *that old guy* again. If she saw him, she might be tempted to tear his hair out for destroying her beautiful garden. That is—if he had any.

I'll settle for kicking him in the shin, she thought angrily.

She twinged with momentary guilt. Kicking an old man seemed like a heartless thing to do. But then, so did destroying her beautiful flowers on the hair-brained idea that she had buried the diamonds under the plants to hide them. But still, that wasn't like her.

Maybe she would settle for yelling at him at the top of her lungs instead.

*　*　*

Stephanie left the boutique that afternoon in a much better mood than when she'd arrived. Though the air was a bit cool today, it was a balmy, sunny day. The golden September sun warmed her face.

She had purchased a new outfit, a burgundy coat dress with brass buttons. Buying something new always lifted her spirits and with her employee discount, the price was often too good to pass up.

She glanced both ways as she left the store with a shopping bag containing the dress wrapped in tissue paper, searching for the stranger who'd been following her, but she saw no sign of him today. Breathing a sigh of relief, she stood at the curb and waited for Shane to pick her up. He pulled up almost immediately, as though he'd been parked nearby. She quickly climbed into the car and shut the door as he sped away.

"Hi!" She smiled as she set her purse and shopping bag on the floor mat. "Are we going to eat first or drive straight to the store?"

Dressed in a navy shirt and jeans, Shane looked rested and in good spirits, so she found it surprising when he suddenly frowned. "Let's drop by the store first. Then we can relax over dinner."

"Sounds good," Stephanie replied. After dealing with Marsha again, she'd be ready for a nice stiff drink to calm her nerves. Something cold and fruity, like Marsha.

Majesty Jewelers occupied the main floor of an old brick building at the south end of the Nicollet Mall in downtown Minneapolis. When they arrived, Stephanie and Shane found the store open but with only one customer browsing the sparkling gems arranged in brightly lit glass cases. Loud, trendy music filled the air.

A female sales rep approached them. She must have been newly hired as Stephanie had never encountered her before today.

"Good afternoon. May I help you?" The slender young woman wore a bright pink designer suit with a white blouse. Her dark hair accented her oval face with a pixie bob. The bejeweled name badge on her lapel read "Abby."

"Hi, Abby," Shane replied. "I'm Shane Kingsley and this is Stephanie Jones. We're looking for Rudy. Is he in today?"

Abby smiled apologetically. "Yes, he is, but he's in a meeting right now and doesn't want to be disturbed."

"How about Marsha?" Stephanie tensed, hoping Marsha had taken today off.

Abby's expression dimmed. "She's in a meeting, too."

Good, Stephanie thought, *we'll just mosey on back to Jock's office to search it and be gone before they find out we were here...*

"No problem," Shane said as he walked toward the offices in the back of the store with Stephanie in tow. "I'm the executor of Jock Tanner's estate and I need to retrieve something from his office. It won't take more than a couple of minutes."

Abby hurried after them. "No, you can't do that! This area is off-limits to anyone but employees!"

Shane ignored her and kept walking.

"Mr. Kingsley! Please stop!" Abby screeched as they reached the doorway to Jock's office.

But it wasn't Jock's office any longer. The space had been thoroughly changed. Jock's possessions were gone and instead, Marsha's IKEA furniture, fuchsia plants, scented candles, and Monet replicas filled the room.

Stephanie looked around in shock and dismay. "What happened to Jock's stuff?"

"It's probably for sale at a thrift store." Shane shook his head. "I knew we should have done this sooner."

Abby stood in the hallway, pounding on Rudy's door. "Mr. Cohen! Mr. Cohen! Open up! We have trespassers! Shane Kingsley and his girlfriend!"

"I'm Jock's fiancée," Stephanie snapped, correcting her. Okay, so Jock hadn't actually gotten around to proposing before his death, but according to Stu, he'd planned to do it so that was good enough for this instance.

A lock clicked on the other side of Rudy's office door then it flew open and Rudy, a short, balding man with black-framed glasses burst out of his office wearing gray slacks and a white shirt. He had a smudge of something red on his chin. "What's going on here?" The moment he saw Shane, he gripped his hands on his hips. "Oh, it *is* you. What do you want?"

Marsha suddenly appeared behind him, straightening the straps on her red dress. Horrified, Stephanie tried not to envision the two of them in a lip-lock, but the picture flitted through her mind anyway, causing her stomach to quake in revulsion.

E-w-w-w...

Shane gestured toward Marsha's scented, floral she-cave. "I wanted to look for something in Jock's office, but it looks like you've already made some changes here. What did you do with Jock's files and his furniture?"

"I turned all of the requested paperwork over to his lawyer and the rest of the stuff is stored in the basement. It's the property of the company," Rudy said placing his hands on his hips. "You want it? Get a court order."

Shane's usual cool manner began to bubble over with anger as his face and neck flushed. "You have no right to interfere with Jock's office until his estate is settled. He still owns half of this business!"

Rudy's eyes narrowed. "I intend to buy the other half, so I

consider the place mine!"

Shane and Rudy stood nose to nose, arguing as Marsha stepped toward Stephanie with a sneer plastered on her face, ignoring the chaos erupting between the men. She gazed critically at Stephanie's cashmere poncho as though the garment was nothing more than a dirty blanket borrowed from her dog's bed.

"Well, well," Marsha said raising one brow as her gaze slid toward Shane, "it didn't take you long to forget about Jock."

"I didn't forget about Jock. For your information, Shane is an old friend, and he just happens to be the executor of Jock's estate, but you already know that. You saw him speak at the funeral." Stephanie had a mind to empty her water bottle over Marsha's head, ruining her Sephora makeup job along with her smug smile, but she simply stared back. "I *could* say the same about you, but I don't need to because the lipstick on Rudy's face says it all." She placed her hand on her throat and gasped in horror. "He's old and wrinkled and bald. And *cranky*. Scraping the bottom of the barrel, aren't we?"

Marsha's amber eyes widened. *"He's rich."* She disdainfully pointed a thumb at Shane. "Unlike your California lover boy, here, who makes a living trying to look and act like someone he's definitely not."

The reference to Shane's stunt-doubling for Dack Reynolds, because he wanted *to be* Dack, was a low blow even for Marsha. "Leave him out of this," Stephanie snapped. "Money isn't everything."

"Oh, yeah?" Marsha's eyes narrowed to slits. "Then give the diamonds back."

"I don't have the diamonds!" Stephanie shouted. "I don't know where they are and frankly, I don't want *anyone* to interrogate me about them ever again!"

Everyone abruptly went silent and stared at her.

"Enough of this." Shane grabbed her hand. "We're leaving."

"Good!" Marsha and Rudy shouted in unison.

Rudy glared at Shane. "My assistant will *see you out.*" He snapped his fingers. "Abby!"

In other words, they were being escorted to make sure they didn't do any damage or steal anything on their way out of the store.

Abby's face paled at Rudy's sharp command. Obviously, she'd never been tasked before with ejecting troublemakers. "This way please," she announced breathlessly.

Shane and Stephanie exchanged angry glances as they silently left the store.

Good riddance…

"Well, that was a total waste of time," Stephanie said with a disappointed sigh.

"I don't think it was a *total* waste," Shane replied as they approached the vehicle. "At least now we know for sure that Rudy has absolutely no sorrow over Jock's death. If he did, he wouldn't have already erased every trace of his business partner from the store and he wouldn't have been so hostile toward me when I asked about it. He's still at the top of my suspect list."

They reached the car. Stephanie stood to one side as Shane unlocked it and opened the door for her. "When he said he *intended* to buy out Jock's half I wondered what he meant," Shane stated. "I know the legal process will take some time, but he seemed anxious about it as though it wasn't a foregone conclusion. I wonder why."

Stephanie slid into the passenger seat and dropped her purse on the floor. "Maybe he's having a difficult time collecting Jock's life insurance."

"That's what I was thinking, too." Shane shut the car door and walked swiftly around to the driver's side.

He got in and started the car. "Where do you want to go for dinner?"

She pulled the seatbelt across her lap. "Why don't we eat somewhere close to my house? I have to let the dog out."

"Okay." Shane pulled into the street and sped away.

Twenty minutes later Shane drove into Stephanie's driveway and shut off the car.

"Maybe I shouldn't go out to eat tonight," Stephanie said solemnly as she unlatched her seatbelt. "I really should get to work and fix my flowerbed." She glanced at her watch. "It's going to be dark in an hour or so and I'm sure it's going to take that long."

He smiled. "I've got a surprise for you. It's done."

"What?"

"After I dropped you off this morning, I went to the hardware store and bought a couple of things to finish the job. I shoveled all the dirt back into place, laid some new landscaping fabric, and added mulch. It looks better than it did before it was disturbed."

"Oh, my gosh," Stephanie replied, overwhelmed with delight. "That's so sweet of you, Shane. I could kiss you!" The words came out before she realized what she'd said, but Shane took obviously them to heart.

He leaned close. "Then why don't you," he whispered in a deep, husky voice. Without waiting for her to respond, he gently placed his lips upon hers. When she didn't resist, he pulled her closer and deepened his kiss.

His action stunned her but in a good way. *He doesn't kiss at all like Jock,* she thought deliriously as her palms began to sweat and her mind spun out of control. *He's...better.*

She slid her arms around his neck and kissed him deeper,

wondering why he hadn't tried this sooner. Perhaps he had a girlfriend in California, or maybe he was being respectful of Jock's memory because he assumed she was still in love with Jock. If so, he was wrong. Dead wrong. That ship had sailed a while ago and sunk somewhere in the sea of infidelity...

Frantic rapping on the window startled them, causing them to jerk apart. Stephanie looked past her shoulder and saw Evelyn with her hands cupped around her eyes, peering through the window.

"Say," she shouted, "someone has been spying on your house all day!"

Chapter Eleven

Stephanie bolted from the car, almost knocking Evelyn backward in the process. "What did you say? Who has been spying on my house?"

Evelyn's rose-print housedress had a dusting of flour smudged across the front. Her short crop of white hair looked mussed, as though she'd been working hard all day in the kitchen.

"A man," she said, placing her hands on her square, stout hips. "An older man with white hair and wire-rimmed glasses. He sat in his car parked at the curb most of the day. I knew he was watching your house. He positioned himself so he could see if anyone arrived through the alley."

Shane walked around the front of the car, staring at the open space between the two houses. "Is he still there?"

Evelyn shook her head. "You just missed him. He drove away about ten minutes ago."

"What kind of car did he drive?"

Evelyn frowned. "I didn't pay much attention to the vehicle. I was more concerned with who was in it, but it was an economy car and it was dark-colored. Plain and brown, I think. Unfortunately, that's all I recall."

"I don't know anyone who drives a brown car," Stephanie remarked, perplexed.

"That settles it." Shane frowned. "I'm spending the night on your porch. The guy has become so brazen he doesn't care who sees him."

Evelyn looked horrified. "My lord, the nights have gotten so cool you'll freeze out there!"

"I'll be fine," Shane said with finality. "I've got a tent and an air mattress and a thermal sleeping bag. If that guy comes back, I'll be ready for him."

"You don't have to go to that extreme," Stephanie argued. "You can stay in my guest bedroom."

"Nope," Shane replied stubbornly. "I'll be too comfortable there and I need to stay focused. I'm not letting him get away again!"

Evelyn brushed the flour from her dress. "Have you kids had your supper?"

"Not yet," Stephanie replied as she grabbed her purse from the car and shut the door. "We were going out to eat but under the circumstances, I think we'd better stay home. We'll probably order a pizza."

"Nonsense!" Evelyn raised her hands, gesturing toward her yard. "You're coming to my house for dinner."

"Thank you, Evelyn, but we don't want you to go to all that trouble," Stephanie said, becoming embarrassed. If she had been alone, she would have accepted. She'd eaten at Evelyn's house many times, but she didn't know if Shane was comfortable with the idea.

Evelyn squeezed her hand. "It's no trouble at all. I just pulled a chicken from the oven, and I was ready to sit down to eat when you arrived. I don't mind setting two more places." She grabbed Shane by the arm. "Come on now. I've got plenty of food."

"Yes, ma'am. Thank you." Shane darted a helpless look at Stephanie as he allowed Evelyn to lead him into her yard.

She followed the pair, her mouth starting to water at the thought of Evelyn's baked chicken and stuffing. She'd had it before and it was delicious. *Finger-lickin'-good* didn't begin to describe Evelyn's chicken dishes.

Evelyn's kitchen reminded Stephanie of an old farmhouse kitchen with pine cupboards painted white, linoleum-covered countertops with a large porcelain sink, and an antique wringer-washing machine stored in the corner—which she still used on a weekly basis. Only the white refrigerator and stove were new. Evelyn pulled up the sides of her Duncan Phyfe drop leaf table and spread out the food while ordering Stephanie to get the additional place settings from the cupboard. Shane was dispatched to get extra chairs from the dining room.

They sat down to a meal of baked chicken, stuffing, mashed potatoes, and gravy, dinner rolls—baked from scratch, of course—and a bowl of home-canned corn. Evelyn had baked an apple crisp for dessert and served it with real whipped cream. All through dinner, she kept the conversation going, asking pointed questions; such as what they had been doing in Stephanie's flower garden. Stephanie kept her answers brief, making it appear that she had decided to rearrange things.

Evelyn also gave Shane the third degree about his job in California and what it was like to work for a famous actor. He answered her questions politely, but Stephanie could tell by his brief answers that he didn't want to talk about himself.

After dinner, Evelyn refused Stephanie's offer to help with the cleanup. "You two run along now. I'll take care of the dishes," she said cheerfully. "Go to a movie or walk to the park. Have some fun together."

They thanked her for a wonderful meal and went back to Stephanie's house.

"Do you think she planned that dinner for us on purpose?" Shane asked once they were in the privacy of her living room. "She had a lot of food on the table for a person who usually eats alone."

Stephanie nodded. "Yep. She's probably been scheming a way to get the three of us together for dinner ever since she saw you sleeping all night in your car in front of the house. She knew I had to come home to let the dog out so she probably watched for us to pull into the driveway. I'll bet she's on the phone giving my mother an update about us right now." Stephanie blushed thinking about Evelyn catching them in the middle of a passionate kiss. Had she noticed? Hmmm…was grass green?

"Evelyn is a nice lady," Shane remarked, "and a great cook. She reminds me of Aunt Bea of Mayberry."

And just as gossipy, too…

Stephanie smiled at his comparison. "She looks out for me like a grandmother. I am so lucky to have a neighbor like her."

"I'm going to make a run home and get my gear," Shane said suddenly. "I'll be back later."

"Before I forget..." Stephanie opened a junk drawer and pulled out a brass key. "Here," she said, offering it to him. "In case of an emergency or if you just need to use the bathroom..."

He slipped the key into his pocket. "Thanks." He hesitated as though he was unsure if he should kiss her again or simply leave. She settled the matter for him by rising on her tiptoes and giving him a smack on the lips.

He smiled as desire shone in his eyes. "I'd better go." grabbing his keys off the counter, he said goodbye and left the house, locking the door behind him.

Stephanie danced into the bathroom and filled the tub for a nice relaxing bubble bath, glowing with more happiness than she'd experienced in a long time. She'd never realized before how miserable she'd been with Jock but spending time with his cousin—who was the exact opposite of him—reminded her of how much fun it could be to hang out with a nice guy and *just be friends*. Life was good.

Well, mostly. They still didn't know who killed Jock and they still didn't know what Jock had done with the diamonds he'd supposedly pilfered from his business. And they still didn't know who was stalking her.

Other than that, things were looking up.

*   *   *

The rumbling of a garbage truck coming down the alley woke Stephanie the next morning. Irritated at being disturbed on her day off, she opened one eye and glanced at the clock.

"Oh, my gosh," she mumbled as she threw off the covers and sat up. "It's nearly ten o'clock! Hobbit needs to be let out!"

She slipped off the bed and stumbled into the kitchen, fully expecting to see a doggie "tootsie roll" on the rug next to the back door, but the rug was clean, and Hobbit lay curled up in his favorite easy chair in the living room. He looked up, disinterested, then went back to sleep.

What the...

Normally he would have been whining to go outdoors. Why wasn't he flying off the chair to greet her?

She went back into the kitchen and peered through the window into the porch. Shane's sleeping bag lay rolled up on a chair. Jock's Navigator wasn't in its usual spot next to the garage.

She smelled the aroma of brewed coffee. Shane must have let himself in and made a pot. He must have taken care of the dog, too.

The handwritten list of suspects and places to investigate lay on the kitchen counter. The jewelry store had been crossed off. The next place awaited their inspection. They were going to Jock's condo today to look for clues. Hopefully, this time they would find something useful.

She'd just finished a late breakfast when she heard a key turn in the lock and Shane appeared in the kitchen. "Hi," he said softly as he slowly walked through the doorway. Stephanie nearly gasped when she saw him. At first, she thought it was Dack Reynolds.

Wow...

Shane wore skin-tight Armand Russo jeans, a grey V-necked t-shirt that emphasized his muscular arms and chest, and Nike sneakers. His Gucci sunglasses were pilot-style with gold metal frames. He gently pulled them off and set them on the countertop.

"Thanks for the coffee." Stephanie held up her favorite Dunoon mug, trying not to stare like a smitten fan. "It was nice to wake up to the aroma of a freshly brewed pot."

Shane opened a cabinet and pulled out a mug. "I would have brought you a cup before I left, but I didn't want to disturb you. I figured the smell would wake you." He poured himself some coffee and leaned against the counter. "Do you still want to go to Jock's condo today?"

"Sure." She sipped her coffee. "You haven't changed your mind, have you?"

"No, of course not." His expression sobered. "I just wanted to make sure you haven't. I'll understand if the place holds too many memories for you and you don't want to revisit them."

She chuckled. "As a matter of fact, it does hold a lot of memories, many of which I don't want to be reminded of, but that's not going to stop me from looking for anything the investigators missed. They don't know Jock like I do. If it's there, I'll spot it. I'm ready to get started whenever you are."

"Good." He drank some coffee and set his cup in the sink. "Let's go."

Chapter Twelve

Jock's condo was in a tall steel and glass building on France Avenue in the affluent community of Edina, Minnesota. Shane pulled out Jock's security card, punched in a code, and entered the building. They walked into a spacious, windowed lobby filled with sofas and chairs in shades of gray. They strode past an open stairway to the second floor as they headed toward the elevators.

"This place has everything," Stephanie said. "On the main floor is an indoor pool, an exercise room, and a daycare center." She pointed to the carpeted double stairway. "Jock used to have football get-togethers up there in the party room. There is also a library and a billiard room."

They entered the elevator and stood quietly as the doors closed. The elevator whisked them up to the tenth floor.

As the doors slowly opened on Jock's floor, Stephanie peered out of the elevator, nervous that one of Jock's neighbors would see them and use the opportunity to ask questions about his death and the status of the investigation. Shane, however, didn't seem to be worried. Perhaps he'd already gone through that with a few of them! He walked straight to Jock's front door, unlocked it, and opened it, standing aside to let Stephanie enter first.

She walked into the condo and stood like a statue in the middle of the living room, quietly observing the place. Everything looked the same as before—the soft cream walls and flax-colored carpet with matching fabric blinds, rust, and cream furniture—but it seemed eerily empty without Jock.

Something inside her nearly compelled her to call out to him, hoping he would walk out of the bedroom in sweatpants and a white t-shirt, his dark hair tousled and a day's growth on his jaw to greet her with his customary grin and a kiss. In her mind, she saw him stretch out on the furniture, resting his stockinged feet on the coffee table with his arms along the back of the sofa.

Why would anyone want to murder him? It was so unfair!

Shane stood behind her, gently sliding his hands over her shoulders. "Are you okay?"

She nodded. "It feels strange to see all of his things but knowing that he no longer lives here."

"Why don't you sit down for a moment and relax? I'll get you a Coke." Shane turned and went into the kitchen. "Would you like a glass with ice?"

"If it's cold, I'll drink it out of the can." She walked over to the window and gazed down at the large, crystal-blue pond behind the building, surrounded by trees, benches, and colorful flowers.

Straighten up. You're here to look for clues leading to a cache of missing diamonds, not dwell on Jock's memory. You're not helping him by wallowing in despair. Get going!

She collapsed into one of the easy chairs opposite the sofa and took a deep breath, determined to push back her feelings and stick to business.

The snap and fizz of a can being opened preceded Shane as he strolled back into the living room with her Coke.

"This hits the spot," Stephanie said in between a couple of generous sips. She stood up, sweeping her hair into a ponytail with an elastic band. "Okay, let's get going. There is something here for us to find. I can feel it in my bones."

They started in the living room, searching through the bookcases. Stephanie could tell the police had been here and gone through Jock's things. Everything was more or less in its usual place, but most of his things had been taken out and put back by people who weren't concerned with neatness and order. She wondered if the crime scene people had discovered anything...

A search of the living room, dining room, and kitchen yielded zero results. Stephanie moved into Jock's study and walked over to his desk. "What is all this?" She pointed toward a stack of brown accordion folders.

"One is filled with everything I've collected on the investigation. The others are holding court filings, invoices, communications from the attorney..."

"Oh," Stephanie said, already losing interest. She searched every nook and cranny in Jock's study and didn't find a thing. "Well, that's that," she said, discouraged as she picked up her Coke can and drank the last drop. "The only places left to look through are the bathroom and the bedroom and I doubt we'll find much in there." She blew stray hairs from her face.

She headed into the bedroom and slid open the closet door, leaving Shane to turn over the mattress and look under it. She busied herself looking through all of Jock's clothing, searching the pockets of his blazers, dress shirts, and hoodies, finding nothing but loose buttons and fast-food receipts. At the end of the row, she stopped in frustration. "I give up!"

"Try once more," Shane said as he lifted the mattress. "This time go the opposite way."

Stephanie started searching through all of the pockets of Jock's clothing again. His navy polyester windbreaker had a small inside pocket that she'd forgotten to check the first time around. When she pulled it open, a business card fell out. She stared at it and did a double-take. "Hey, look at this…"

Shane left what he was doing and approached her. "What is it?"

She grabbed a tissue to keep from getting her prints on it and used the tissue to pick it up. It read "Meet me tonight. Same time, same place."

Shane silently stared at the plain white card with the words written in all capital letters. He flipped it over to check the back. It was blank. He looked up. "Do you happen to remember the last time Jock wore this windbreaker?"

Stephanie nodded. "About two weeks before his death. He wore it to the lake to check on the boat because it had stormed all day. He could have worn it after that." She stared at the card. "This looks like one of those cards you fill out at the florist shop. Someone must have sent him flowers to get this message to him." She checked the windbreaker again. "But there is no envelope. He must have tossed that."

Shane handed the tissue with the card back to her. "It looks like a woman's handwriting. Why didn't she just call him on the phone?"

"Anything electronic can be traced," Stephanie replied, "and she obviously didn't want me to know she was having an affair with him."

They looked at each other. "Marsha," they said aloud in unison.

Stephanie folded up the tissue with the card inside it and smacked it on the dresser. "That woman is a traitor of the worst kind." She shrugged. "Whatever. I'm not looking back."

Shane slipped his arms around her and held her close. "I'm sorry you went through so much with my cousin, Stephanie. I promise I'll make it up to you somehow—"

Suddenly the front door opened and the voices of two women echoed through the condo. Shane quickly backed away and began straightening the covers on Jock's bed as Stephanie slid the tissue-wrapped card into her pocket.

Footsteps padded on the carpet, and they were coming straight toward the bedroom.

Shane did the best he could to pull the covers into place and straighten them just as a woman came into the doorway, filling the air with her strong perfume. "Aunt Pat, what are you doing here?"

Patricia Tanner looked like she'd just come from the salon. Her dark, shoulder-length hair with a center part didn't have a strand out of place. She wore beige tweed slacks and a beige sweater. Her dark-eyed, suspicious gaze slid from him to Stephanie and back to him again. "I came to put some documents from the funeral home in your files." She glanced at the rumpled bed and then back at Shane. "What are *you* doing here?"

"Um…we were looking for anything that the crime scene techs might have missed to give us a clue as to where Jock hid those diamonds—"

"That's not your job," Pat retorted. "Leave it to the detectives on the case."

"Mom, who are you talking to?" Amelia Tanner appeared in the doorway. Jock's twenty-five-year-old sister wore jeans and a red plaid top, her straight dark hair falling to her waist. Her deep-set brown eyes, fringed with thick black lashes widened at seeing Stephanie and Shane together—in Jock's bedroom. "Hi, Stef. Hi, Shane."

Stephanie stepped forward, smiling. "Hi, Amelia! It's been a long time since we've spoken. I saw you at the funeral but didn't get a chance to talk to you." All through the funeral, Amelia had so many supportive friends surrounding her that Stephanie couldn't get close to speak to her.

Amelia grinned at Shane. "Hey, did I hear you say that you're hunting for the missing diamonds? Amateur detectives! That's cool!"

Patricia glared at Stephanie in disbelief. "Is this what you were really searching for?" She reached under the bed and pulled out a blush pink baby doll negligee. The sheer, pleated garment was made with georgette fabric. A wide satin ribbon connected the skirt to the triangular lace cups and spaghetti straps.

Stephanie gawked at the sexy nightgown, her face and neck heating up with embarrassment. "Tha—that's not mine."

Patricia shoved it toward her, not buying her denial. "Take it and be on your way."

"*Mom*," Amelia countered with embarrassment, "don't you remember who this is? Stephanie is Jock's fiancée. He introduced her to us at Jason's wedding."

Patricia folded her arms, her combative stance indicating she thought of Stephanie as merely an opportunistic fortune hunter. A lowly sales assistant chasing after a wealthy jeweler. "He never said anything to me about getting married."

"Well, he told me about it," Amelia argued emphatically. "A couple of days before he died, he called me and said he and Stephanie were getting married in Vegas at the Bellagio." She looked at Stephanie. "Was that still the plan at the time of his death?"

You knew too? Stephanie thought miserably. *Just how many people were in on his little secret?*

"Yeah." Her head bobbed like a marionette on a string. "Next month."

Pat stared at Stephanie's hands. "Where is your engagement ring?"

"Well, um..." Stephanie cleared her throat. "He was in the

process of designing one for me, but unfortunately, he never got the chance to finish it."

Patricia left the room, indicating they were dismissed.

Amelia followed them to the front door. "Call me later, Shane. Let's get together soon. Bye, Stef! It was great seeing you again!" She stopped at the door. "Hey, did you check Jock's locker at the yacht club? I doubt you'll find anything there, but it's worth a try."

Shane waved goodbye. "That's next on our list."

Stephanie stepped into the elevator with the tissue-wrapped card in her pocket and fumed all the way down to the lobby. When the doors opened, she stormed out, charging toward the entrance.

"Don't take it personally," Shane called after her as he followed her. "Aunt Pat comes across as rude to everybody. That's just her way."

Once they were outside, Stephanie headed toward the nearest trash receptacle. "I'm not mad at your aunt. I don't care what she thinks of me. I'm angry that Marsha deliberately left this under Jock's bed for me to find!" She shoved the nightgown into the trash and spun around. "He was cheating on me at the same time he was planning to elope with me! What a fool I've been. I wish I'd never met Jock Tanner!"

But she had—and now she was being stalked by someone who might have murdered him. She had to keep searching for the diamonds and ultimately uncover who wanted to take them from her.

Her life depended on it.

Chapter Thirteen

"Where are we going?" Stephanie asked curiously as the SUV sped away from Jock's condominium building. She pointed toward the west in the direction of Lake Minnetonka. "The Yacht club is *that* way."

"We're going to a favorite place of mine to get ice cream," Shane replied, focusing on the road. "I don't blame you for being upset. I'd be mad at Jock, too, if I were in your place, but it's got you all worked up and I can't think of a better way to calm you down." He cut her a sideways glance. "This place makes great malts and shakes. Especially hot fudge. You game?"

Yum…I'm calming down already.

She laughed. "Now you've done it. I'm dying for hot fudge."

He stepped on the gas. "Good, we're on our way."

Twenty minutes later they sat in a wooden booth with a red and white checkered tablecloth, devouring fountain glasses filled with thick hot fudge malts. Shane dipped his long-handled spoon into his malt can, scooped up creamy malt and whipped cream, and held it to Stephanie's lips. "Feeling better now?"

"*Definitely.*" She licked the cold sweet treat off the spoon. Shane was right. She needed to calm down so she could think clearly. They had important work to do. "Are you still planning to drive out to the yacht club today?"

"Yeah." He checked his watch. "Hopefully, we'll get out of there before rush hour. The traffic on the freeway is bumper-to-bumper all afternoon, but rush hour is total gridlock."

*   *   *

King's Marina and Yacht Club spanned over six natural lakefront acres surrounded by a sprawling neighborhood of large homes, lush gardens, and towering mature trees. Stephanie and Shane arrived to find a small traffic jam in the marina's parking lot of SUVs and pickups pulling boats on trailers. Shane slowed the SUV as he pulled in, driving cautiously to maneuver around a John Deere tractor hauling a large yacht. They parked their vehicle in a far corner and walked to the main building.

The late September sun sparkled like diamonds on the rippling sapphire water across the huge expanse of King's Bay. Stephanie slipped on her sunglasses and scanned the marina for Jock's boat. It was there, moored in his slip. Seeing it again gave her an instant shiver. The last time she'd been on that boat…

Inside the clubhouse, they approached the main counter to sign in to access the lockers. Jock kept a locker year-round so he could jog along the lake and use the clubhouse showers during the months when his boat was in storage.

A teenager with long blonde hair in loose spiral curls stood behind the counter wearing a deep blue polo shirt bearing an embroidered gold crown—the King's Marina logo—greeting customers and answering questions.

Shane approached her and set a folder on the counter. "I'm the executor of Jock Tanner's estate and I'd like to clean out his locker."

The teen's face paled, her blue eyes widening at the mention of

Jock's name. "I—I'll have to ask my supervisor about that. I don't know if anyone other than the family is allowed to access it."

Shane opened his file and removed a document encased in a sheet protector. "This gives me permission to act on behalf of the family."

She scanned it—front and back then compared his signature to the one on his driver's license. "I need to show this to my supervisor. May I take it?"

He pulled off his sunglasses and flashed her a megawatt smile. "Of course. Do whatever you need to do."

She disappeared for a few minutes and returned with an older, heavyset woman called Marge. Short and gray-haired, Marge carried her tortoiseshell glasses on a beaded chain around her neck. She handed the document back to him. "Here you are, Mr. Kingsley. Do you know the combination to the lock?" She clasped her hands together. "If not, I'm afraid there isn't anything I can do to assist you on that. As long as the rent is paid, we're not allowed to tamper with it."

Shane turned to Stephanie with a questioning look. Obviously, he didn't know the combination and hadn't anticipated beforehand that there would be an issue with one.

"Yes," Stephanie offered quickly. She couldn't think of it offhand, but maybe going back to the locker room would jog her memory. "Yes, we do."

At least, I hope we do…

Marge tapped her finger on a clipboard containing the day's roster. "You'll have to sign in. Both of you."

Shane picked up the pen attached to the clipboard by a string and was about to sign his name when he froze.

Curious, Stephanie wondered what had caused him to pause like that. She leaned close to read the roster—and froze, too.

"Mrs. Tanner" had signed the roster twenty minutes ago. What was Pat Tanner doing here? She must have heard Shane telling Amelia they were stopping by the yacht club, but why did she feel the need to get here first?

They signed the roster then Stephanie led Shane back to Jock's locker. She'd been here with Jock many times but hadn't paid much attention to the lock combination. He'd spoken it aloud on several occasions. She should have paid attention!

Mrs. Tanner was nowhere to be seen, but the heavy scent of sandalwood perfume still lingered in the air. Had she taken everything out of the locker and split or did Jock's combination lock prevent her from getting into it?

Each heavy-duty steel locker had two compartments. Jock's compartment was the upper one.

Shane stood aside. "Do your magic."

She grabbed the lock. "I can't exactly remember the combination."

Shane leaned one hand against the locker, frowning with irritation. "Stephanie, you said you knew what it was!"

"Well…" She spun the dial. "It was a specific date. I remember that much. If I could only remember what that date was for!"

Shane sighed. "I don't suppose it was his birthday…"

"No. It was something more important than that."

"Your birthday?"

She folded her arms in frustration. Some detectives they were! Amateur didn't begin to describe their incompetence! "I wish! Oh, it's so frustrating. Think, Stephanie! Think!" She stared at the ceiling and tapped her foot. "It had something to do with his boat." She gasped. "The day he bought it, maybe? He'd just acquired a space in the marina the same week we started dating. I remember him telling me how he'd pulled some strings and got to the top of the waitlist. It only took him two weeks to get a slip."

They stared at each other as realization dawned. Marge could give them those dates…

They practically ran back to the customer counter, both firing questions at Marge at once. Ten minutes later, they were back with a list of possible dates acquired from Jock's application to the marina. The third date on the list worked—the date he acquired the slip. *Like, duh!*

If they were excited to finally get it open, the contents inside dashed their spirits. All they found were smelly clothes and tennis shoes. And a brand-new pair of monogrammed socks. *Huh?*

Stephanie held them up for Shane to inspect. "Jock didn't buy these. He would never go to all the trouble to get his socks monogrammed. A sock was a sock as far as he was concerned."

Shane looked them over with curiosity. "A gift, perhaps, from someone?"

Stephanie snatched them from his hands and threw them back into the locker. "*Obviously*. But I can't see Marsha going to all that trouble. All she thinks about is herself."

"Hmmm…" Shane pulled out all of the items and shoved them into a reusable King's Marina shopping bag Marge had sold to him for five dollars. "I can. I think she would if she wanted to impress him."

They emptied the locker and left the building. On the way back to the car, Shane stopped. "Let's go check out the boat. It's the next item on our list anyway."

Stephanie balked, not wanting to step foot in that thing ever again. At least, not until she'd had time to prepare herself. "But you said you wanted to avoid rush hour. If we waste time searching the boat today, the traffic on the freeway will be slower and more congested than this parking lot."

Shane shoved his folder into the bag with Jock's clothes and grabbed her hand. "It doesn't make sense to drive back here later. It won't take long. Come on."

"Don't we have to check with Detective Garrett first?" she argued, trying to stall him. "Isn't it still a crime scene?"

"The boat was cleared by the police before it was returned to the marina," Shane said as they headed toward the docks. "I hired a specialized company to clean it up once it was transported back here. It's ready to list for sale."

Dreading this part of their investigation, she dragged her feet all the way to the dock.

Chapter Fourteen

Stephanie followed Shane along the wide wooden dock, apprehensive about returning to the place of Jock's murder. She would have never gone back to the boat alone, and didn't want to be there now, but understood it was necessary. If Jock hid the diamonds on his boat, they needed to find them. Shane's presence gave her the encouragement she needed to face her fear and get the job done.

Boats of all shapes and sizes were moored to the dock on both sides. They passed several large cruisers before they came upon the *Misty Blue*, Jock's cabin cruiser. The white Sea Ray Sundancer with a grayish-blue stripe was long and sleek, glistening majestically in the afternoon sun.

They went up the small steps on the transom to the cockpit, the open area on the back of the boat where Jock used to entertain friends and clients. The outdoor party room was equipped with a bar, a refrigerator, and a built-in grill. She stood behind Shane, nervously waiting for him to unlock the door to the cabin below. Her heart began to thunder at the clicking sound as his key turned in the lock. He opened the narrow door and descended the stairs.

She reluctantly followed behind him, stopping in the main room of the cabin. To her, it was the kitchen, but Jock said it was called "the salon." Behind the stairway was the entertainment center—a sunken living room with a television, a coffee table that served as both a bench and a storage box, and a white leather sofa that converted to a guest bed.

Every counter and appliance shone like a mirror from the good work of the professional cleaning crew. Every cabinet and shelf had been emptied. The air contained a strong odor of disinfectant.

The door to Jock's bedroom hung slightly ajar. She averted her gaze as quickly as possible, but not before accidentally catching a glimpse of the bed. The one he was lying on when she found him. *Murdered.*

She didn't know if her reaction was triggered by the strong odor or the strong memories, but she suddenly couldn't breathe. She had to get out of there to catch her breath.

"Shane," she whispered, barely able to speak. "I need my phone." She'd forgotten it in the car when they went into the clubhouse. "I left it in the car on the charger."

His deep blue eyes perused hers with concern. "Do you want me to get it for you?"

"No, no," she protested. "I'll go. It won't take me long. On the way back, I'll get us each a can of Coke from the vending machine. There's one outside the back door of the clubhouse."

He handed her the SUV's key fob. "Okay. Take your time. I'll go through the bedroom while you're gone."

She grabbed a wad of money from her purse along with the fob and hurried out of the cabin, not bothering to shut the door behind her as she rushed up the steps. Drawing in a deep breath, she shoved the cash into her jeans pocket as she walked across the cockpit and descended the stairs on the transom to step on the dock. The soft glow of the sun warmed her shoulders. A slight breeze filled her lungs with the fishy aroma of lake air. Most of the trees had reached their peak of fall color and the surrounding oaks provided a rich tapestry of wine, gold, and burnt orange hues.

By the time she reached the car, her anxiety had subsided. The parking lot was quiet now; many of the vehicles were gone. She grabbed her phone in its pink wallet case and turned it on, preoccupied with it while she walked to the vending machine. She heard the voices of two teen boys and looked up. They veered toward her on their bicycles but she didn't think anything of it until one of them nearly ran her down. He reached out and grabbed her phone in the process.

"Hey!" she shouted as she collided with the bike and knocked it over. "What's the matter with you? Give me back my phone!"

The tall, dark-haired kid riding the bike dropped his foot on the ground to steady himself and avoid falling off, but by that time, Stephanie had slammed against him, screaming and knocking him off balance. They lay on the ground, playing tug-of-war over her phone as the other teen circled them, jeering at her and encouraging his accomplice to finish the job.

"Someone's comin'!" the other teen shouted as he sped away. "C'mon, we gotta go!"

Suddenly, large hands reached over her shoulder and grabbed the phone, ripping it out of their grip. Then the hands gently pulled her upright.

At the same time, the would-be thief scrambled to his feet and picked up his bike, wheeling away as fast as he could.

"Don't come back!" The deep, commanding voice was threaded with a protective, fatherly tone. "You'll be sorry you did!"

Stephanie turned to thank the man for intervening and nearly swallowed her tongue. It was the same man who had been following her since the day she glimpsed him watching her in the bookstore. He was medium height with short, white hair under his brown bill cap. Wire-rimmed glasses framed gentle green eyes. "Y—you? What are you doing here? Why are you following me?"

"I'm not following you. I'm protecting you." He examined the long scrape on her arm. "You'd better get that cleaned up right away and put some antiseptic on it. I've got a small first aid kit in my car. It will work for a temporary fix but you may need to bandage it with gauze when you get home."

She had no idea when or how the scrape happened, but it must have been when she pulled her attacker to the ground. Her injury, however, was the last thing on her mind. "You're protecting me? Why? Who hired you?"

The man extended his hand. "I'm Arthur Gale, a private investigator. I'm working for Jock Tanner."

Stephanie nearly fainted.

*   *   *

"Shane!" Stephanie thundered down the stairs as she burst into the cabin carrying the Coke cans. "Shane, come here!"

Shane appeared in the bedroom doorway, shutting it behind him. "What's wrong? Did somebody break into the car?"

"No. Nothing like that. I want you to meet someone." She turned back to the door just as Arthur Gale filled it with his broad-shouldered frame. "This is Arthur Gale, the man who has been following me. And guess what? The night I saw him in the bookstore at the festival, he was waiting there for Jock. He's a private investigator!"

Shane's jaw literally dropped as he watched the man descend the stairway.

"Hi," Arthur Gale's deep voice boomed in a friendly manner as he extended his free hand. The other one held a cold can of Sprite. "You must be Shane Kingsley. Glad to meet you."

Shane warily shook hands with him. "Would you mind telling me what this is all about? Why are you following Stephanie? And why are you still working for Jock? He's been dead for weeks."

Stephanie set the Coke cans on the table and pulled up a chair for their visitor. "Let's all sit down. I have a feeling this is going to take a while."

Shane stared with alarm at her bloody scrape. "What happened to you?"

"I fell down," Stephanie said, staring at the damage done to her arm. "I'd better clean it up. I'll be right back."

A couple of minutes later she emerged from the bathroom. The cuts had been cleaned and rubbed with antiseptic ointment from the first aid kit on the boat. While cleaning her wound, she'd listened to Arthur Gale recount the incident in the parking lot.

"Let's talk about Jock. Perhaps you should start at the beginning, Mr. Gale," Shane remarked suspiciously as Stephanie took her seat next to him.

"Just call me Art," the man replied and opened his soda can with a loud snap. "I was initially hired by Jock to tail his partner, Rudy Cohen. Jock suspected Rudy of stealing money from the business and he wanted me to find out everything I could about Rudy's lifestyle. Jock had his accountant going over the books with a fine-toothed comb and I was to tail the ba—" Art cleared his throat. "I mean…Mr. Cohen. The job ended, of course, when Jock was killed, but he'd given me such a hefty retainer that I decided I'd work off the rest by keeping a close watch on Miss Jones."

"Um…Stephanie," she said, stunned. "Am I a suspect?"

Art laughed. "No, of course not. But Jock told me he'd left the diamonds he'd acquired with you to keep them safe. I knew it wouldn't be long before the vulture who killed him figured it out and began circling you, so I reckoned you needed protection."

What??

"No," Stephanie shook her head vehemently. "I don't have the diamonds and I don't know what happened to them. Shane and I have been searching everywhere to find clues as to what he did with them. That's what we're doing now." She visibly shivered. "Turning over the cabin to see if there is anything the crime scene guys missed."

Art took a swig of his soda. "Did you find it, then?"

Shane and Stephanie stared at each other in confusion then leaned forward blurting out simultaneously, "Find *what*?"

Art set down his soda can and pushed his chair back. He pulled a small remote from his pocket, about the size of a stick of gum, and pressed a button on it. Something in the entertainment room made a clicking sound. He went into the room and opened a narrow storage compartment along the back framework of the white leather sofa. "Yep, it's still here." He pulled out a collection of papers and brought them back to the table. "I should have told the police about this when they interrogated me, but I swore to Jock that if anything happened to him, I'd protect the information until I could turn it over to his administrator." Art nodded at Shane as he opened a large piece of paper. "This is for you."

Shane stared at the paper unfolded on the table. "It looks like a plat map."

"It is," Art replied as he pointed to the fact that it was situated along France Avenue. "Jock acquired this parcel a couple of weeks before his death. Next spring, he was going to build his own jewelry store. That's why he was putting aside those diamonds. He wanted out of his partnership because he knew it was just a matter of time before the business went bankrupt."

"So, that's what happened to all of his investments and CDs,"

Shane exclaimed with a whistle as he perused the document. "He must have shelled out a lot of cash for it."

Art tapped his finger on the map. "That piece of land is in a prime location. Even undeveloped, it's worth a fortune."

Shane looked up. "How did you end up with the remote? You were here—on the boat—the night Jock was killed, weren't you?"

"Yes, I was." Art reached into his pocket and placed the remote on the table, pushing it toward Shane. "Jock called me and said he'd driven his boat to the public marina in Wayzata and he wanted me to meet him there. He was worried about you, Stephanie. Marsha Goodwin had been making threats against you. So, yeah, I was with him on the boat the night he was murdered, but Jock was still alive when I left him. Before I left, we agreed to meet again, with you, the next night at the bookstore after Stephanie went off with her friends." He gripped the table, his knuckles turning white. "Rudy showed up just as I was leaving, and he was in a foul mood. Jock slipped the remote to me to keep it safe and I've had it ever since."

Stephanie sipped her Coke, but it had no taste. She grimaced. "Do you know who else came to see Jock that night?"

Art's thick brows knit together. "Marsha Goodwin visited him before me. She was leaving just as I arrived at the dock. There were a lot of people milling about so she didn't notice me, but I noticed her. She was fuming. He'd just dumped her and told her that he was going to marry you."

Of course, she knew—didn't everyone? Except for me and his mother!

"I can imagine the tantrum she must have had," Shane scoffed.

Art responded with a cynical laugh. "Marsha has the personality of a rabid wolverine. That woman is power-hungry. She's not happy just to be part of the show. She wants to *run* the show." He nodded at

Stephanie. "She was spitting tacks that night, I tell you. She's always been green with jealousy over you."

Stephanie considered Art's words. "Do you think she killed him?"

Art shrugged. "I wouldn't put it past her to have gone back to see him again after the festival closed down for the night. When she didn't get the answer she wanted, she probably lost her temper and stabbed him. She certainly had a motive. But then, so does Rudy." He took another swig of soda. "There was one other person Jock was supposed to meet with that night…his accountant, Stu Hale."

"Stu and Jock were good friends," Stephanie said. "I saw Stu at the funeral. He seemed genuinely sad about Jock's death."

"I'm not so sure about that," Art warned. "When it comes to money, Stu's a tightwad, but his ex-wife spends his dough like it's going out of style. He's desperate to get back together with her so even though he threatens to cut her off, he keeps giving her more. Consequently, he's broke. He comes across as a nice guy, but frankly, I think he'd do anything to get her back. *Anything*…"

Art glanced at his watch. "Well, kids, I need to get going." He stood and pulled his wallet from his front pocket. "It's been nice meeting you both. Here's my business card," he said and placed two cards on the table. "Give me a call if you need anything. In the meantime," he grinned, "I'll be close by."

They thanked him and said goodbye as he went up the stairs.

"That was interesting," Shane said after Art left. "Now we know who has been following you, and we know without a doubt who is desperate to get their hands on the diamonds, but we still don't know where the diamonds are." He looked down at the map of Jock's property and let out a deep sigh. "And now this… Things just keep getting more complicated."

Chapter Fifteen

Cold, dark clouds greeted the first day of October. The wind whipped Stephanie's hair around her face, chilling her to the bone as she waited at the bus stop after work to catch a ride home. It would have been nice to get a lift from Shane, but she hadn't seen him for several days. He was busy helping his dad paint their house and garage.

They'd gone through every place on their list that they suspected Jock could have hidden the diamonds, and though they'd encountered some interesting things—like meeting Arthur Gale—they still had no idea what Jock had done with them.

She tried to read an eBook on her phone on the bus ride home but couldn't concentrate. Shane would be going back to California soon and then she'd be on her own. Could she solve this problem by herself? So far, it looked impossible, no matter how much help she had.

Hobbit met her at the front door, twirling around in his happy dance to see her. She tossed her purse on the sofa and dropped her unopened mail on the dining room table on her way to the kitchen. When she opened the back door for Hobbit to do his business in the backyard, she glanced across her property. What was left of her beautiful flowers was fading fast. The metro area hadn't received its first hard frost of the year yet, but the weatherman had predicted it was coming later this week.

Then her garden would be finished for the season, and she would have to put away all of her yard ornaments.

She loved everything about fall—pumpkin patches, apple orchards, hot spiced cider, and the trees turning rich, bold colors—but the thought of another dark and dreary winter that inevitably followed made her sad.

Maybe I should take a vacation somewhere sunny and warm…

It sounded like a great plan except for one pesky detail; she didn't have money for travel. Every dollar she could spare had to be spent on repairs to her aging home.

After Hobbit returned to the house and gobbled his tablespoon of canned dog food along with his dry food, Stephanie made herself a cup of hot chocolate and went into the living room to warm up and relax. She grabbed the stack of mail on her way and curled up on the sofa to look through it. As usual, the mail consisted of mostly ads and letters from politicians asking for donations, and one from Town and Country Life Insurance Company. She nearly tossed it aside with all of the other junk mail destined for the trash, but something prompted her to take another look. It wasn't bulk mailed and was addressed directly to her.

Hmmm…

She ripped it open and found a letter addressed to her regarding a claim on an insurance policy.

What claim? This is a mistake. The insurance company must have gotten my name in error somehow. It should have been directed to Rudy.

But the letter indicated that the company was notifying her to inform her that their claim process had changed and was now completely electronic. In order to file a claim, she needed to set up an account and verify her eligibility then fill out the proper fields to start the application process.

She stared at the letter and blinked, thoroughly confused.

What does this mean? That—that I'm the beneficiary of Jock's life insurance?

She swallowed hard. No, that couldn't be right...

She sat back and stared at the ceiling, remembering how Rudy had acted toward her both at the funeral and when she'd showed up at the store with Shane. He'd seemed angry toward her. Perhaps he'd already found out the hard way that Jock had changed his beneficiary—by getting shut out by the insurance company.

The letter fluttered to the floor as she processed the information. Given what she knew about Jock's plans for a new store, he could have decided to secretly change the beneficiary, but if so, why didn't he tell her what he'd done?

Maybe he had so much on his mind with the audit, cashing in his investments, and the land sale that he forgot to tell her. Of course, it didn't help that he had a jealous girlfriend on the side that he was trying to break up with.

Yep, he definitely had piled his plate high...

On a whim, she snatched the letter off the floor and went into the spare bedroom where she had her computer set up on a small desk. She booted it up and found the insurance company on the internet then proceeded according to the instructions to set up an account. To her disappointment, she hit a roadblock right away when the application needed two things she didn't have—the policy number and a certified copy of the death certificate.

She leaned backward in her chair and ran her fingers through her tangled, windblown hair. "Darn! Now, what do I do? I don't have that information!"

Yeah, but I know who does...

Shane had said he'd kept all of Jock's legal papers in the accordion files on Jock's desk. For a moment, she considered calling

Shane and telling him what she needed, but in the back of her mind, she realized it was best not to get him involved. If word of her expected inheritance somehow got out, it could create problems with Rudy and possibly Pat Tanner as well. Shane might even be accused of corroborating with her to get Jock's money. Yes, it was best to keep this to herself. For the time being, anyway.

That said, she still needed the information to file the claim and without Shane's help, there was only one way to get it. She'd have to sneak into Jock's condo and find it.

She made sure she had the login and password written down and had bookmarked the insurance company's website before she closed out the page on her computer. Then she looked up the bus schedules to get to Jock's condo and back home. Yes, she could do it, but she had to get moving.

She quickly changed into sweatpants, a turtleneck shirt, and a hoodie, all black. She slipped on a pair of black suede ankle boots with rubber soles, grabbed her phone, a bus card, some money, and the items she needed to get into Jock's condo. She locked up on her way out, leaving a couple of lights on in the house, and ran four blocks to Johnson Street to catch the bus going downtown to the Nicollet Mall. On the mall, she'd transfer to another bus that would drop off close to Jock's condominium complex.

Ninety minutes later, Stephanie trudged across the brightly lit parking lot of Jock's condominium building. She nervously pulled out her security card and swiped the card reader, hoping Jock's death hadn't prompted the security team to change the code. If they did, her mission was over before it started. But to her amazement, the reader accepted the card, and the door unlocked. Hallelujah! She pushed it open and walked across the lobby, keeping her head down as she made a beeline for the elevator.

The elevator doors opened. Thankfully, the car was empty. She entered it and punched the button for the tenth floor, crossing her fingers that she would make it into the condo without a problem. When the elevator whisked open on Jock's floor, she stuck her head out to gauge the situation. The hallway was deserted. She walked swiftly to his unit and tried her key in the door. *It worked.* Why hadn't they changed the locks and the security code? Was it because Pat Tanner didn't want the inconvenience of getting new keys and a reprogrammed card?

She moved quickly through the condo, turning on lights as she passed through the entryway and the living room. The faint scent of Pat Tanner's perfume lingered in every room reminding her that Pat had a key and could show up unexpectedly. She needed to get her business taken care of and get out of there as quickly as possible.

In the study, she found the folders Shane had referred to on Jock's desk and began sifting through them. It didn't take long to find the death certificate—there were multiple copies—but she couldn't find anything referring to the life insurance policy.

Suddenly, loud voices echoed in the corridor. She froze. Did the security team catch her on camera and dispatch someone to check her out? She stopped and waited, sweating profusely as her heart pounded in her chest, hoping it was just a couple of the other tenants having a conversation.

Out in the hallway, a door slammed, and the voices stopped. Breathing a sigh of relief, Stephanie riffled through Jock's file cabinet, looking for his insurance policy. After a long and frustrating fifteen minutes, she found the policy in the bottom drawer mixed in with outdated household insurance papers. She shut the cabinet, folded the pages, and shoved them into her waistband along with the death certificate. Then as quickly and as quietly as she could, she turned off all the lights and left the condo.

She didn't allow herself to relax until she'd boarded the bus on France Avenue bound for downtown Minneapolis where she would transfer to the Johnson Street line. It would be a long ride home, but the effort had been worth it.

Stephanie didn't arrive home until quite late, but as soon as she entered the house, she let the dog out for a quick piddle and then went straight to her computer to finish setting up her application with Town and Country Life Insurance Company.

Slowly, she went through the process, making sure all the fields were filled out accurately and a copy of the death certificate was correctly uploaded. Then she saved it and logged out. An email promptly appeared, verifying that she had completed the process and would be notified in the next seven to ten days as to the status of her claim.

She stared at the computer for a long time, stunned. This whole day had been surreal, to say the least. She was glad she'd decided not to tell anyone about the money. At least not until she knew for sure her claim was approved—and then she would only tell her parents. She *really* wanted to tell Shane but knew she needed to exercise patience and see the process through first.

In the meantime, all she could do was wait.

Chapter Sixteen

On Monday morning, Shane called to let Stephanie know he was finished with the painting job and asked if it was a good time to drop by to see her. She had the day off from the boutique and was busy mowing her lawn for the last time of the season when the SUV pulled into the driveway.

"I'll finish this for you," he hollered over the motor of the lawnmower. "I'll join you in the house in a couple of minutes."

"Okay, thanks!" She handed the mower over to him and went into the house, happy to get out of the chore that always turned her snow-white tennis shoes into variegated shades of green.

She had an ice-cold Coke ready for him along with a bowl of chips and French onion dip when he appeared in the kitchen.

"I put your mower back in the garage," he said as he dug a large ripple chip into the dip.

"Great, thanks." Stephanie joined him at the table and grabbed a chip from the bowl. "How did you like painting the house?"

He rolled his eyes. "Boring."

"Yeah, but you saved your dad a lot of money by doing it

yourselves," Stephanie said as she munched on a thick chip.

Shane shrugged. "Dad's too cheap to hire a professional for something like that. He insists on doing it himself."

Stephanie laughed. "That sounds like *my* dad!"

Shane reached into his jeans pocket and pulled out a square, white envelope. He tossed it on the table. "Did you get one of these?"

Stephanie wiped her fingers on a napkin and picked up the envelope. She drew out a square card made with stiff white paper. It was an invitation from Valerie Hale, inviting Shane to an outdoor reception next Saturday at noon to honor Jock Tanner. "No, I didn't." She turned over the envelope to see the postmark. "When did you receive it?"

Shane set down his Coke. "On Saturday, but I didn't see it until today. My parents got one, too. My mom said it's an informal reception for Jock's inner circle because the family didn't have one after the funeral."

Stephanie dropped the invitation on the table. "Well, I'm not family so I don't qualify."

He grabbed her hand. "You're coming as my date."

"No, Shane." She shook her head. "It would be awkward for me."

"Hey," he argued. "Rudy and Stu are invited and they're not family so why not you too? According to Aunt Pat, about forty people are invited. Jock's closest family, friends, and associates."

"Obviously, ex-girlfriend and almost-a-bride don't count." She exhaled a tense breath. "I don't know about this…"

"Hey," he said with an upbeat note in his voice as he picked up a chip. He scooped up a mound of dip with it and held it to her lips. "There's no telling what might happen when you get all of those people together. One of them could be a murderer and it just might be our only chance to find out who it is."

Stephanie chewed slowly, buying time to come up with an answer. She didn't want to crash that party and smile like she cared or make friendly conversation with people to try to get information out of them because she didn't want to be an amateur detective any longer. They'd tried everything they could think of to find those diamonds and who murdered Jock, but they'd come up empty-handed every time. It just seemed like another exercise in futility.

But she could tell by the stubborn look on his face that he wasn't about to take no for an answer. She sighed. "Okay. I don't think it will do any good, but I'll give it one more shot."

He took her hand. "What's wrong?"

Her shoulders sagged. "I'm tired of looking for a needle in a haystack."

"We know a lot more about the situation than when we started," Shane argued. "Look at all the information we got from Art. We were so wrong about him."

Discouraged, she rested her chin on the heel of her hand. "He was wrong, too. He insisted that Jock gave me the diamonds, but I've turned my house and garage upside down. They're not here!"

Shane lifted his gaze. "What about up there?" He pointed toward the attic access in the ceiling. "Did you look there?"

"Are you kidding me?" Stephanie let out a cynical chuckle. "All you'll find up there is dusty old insulation and mouse poop."

Shane stood, ignoring her excuses. "I'll get your stepladder from the garage." He returned quickly and set up the ladder. She watched him remove the panel and climb up higher so he could see clearly into the attic. "I need a flashlight."

She grabbed one from a junk drawer in the kitchen and stood below the ladder in boredom, waiting for him to satisfy his curiosity and come back down.

He handed her back the flashlight then came down the ladder holding a shoebox.

"What's that?" Stephanie stared at the box. "I've never seen it before."

"It has barely any dust on it so it hasn't been there long," he replied excitedly. He brought it to the table and lifted the lid. It contained a stack of photographs. He took them out and whistled in surprise as he sifted through them.

Stephanie craned her neck to see the photos but he kept them out of reach. "Who is it?"

His eyes widened. "I don't know, but she's totally nude."

What??

"Let me see!" She snatched one away from him and stared at it, trying to make sense of the photo. It was a nude woman all right, but the part showing her head had been torn from the picture. She gasped as her face and neck heated with embarrassment at the racy images that left absolutely *nothing* to the imagination. "Why is her head missing? Do you think she's dead?"

Shane shook his head and turned the photograph to look at it from another angle. "The pose indicates she's very much alive. I suspect these photos were used to taunt or threaten someone using the very thing she doesn't want the world to see."

Stephanie grabbed the rest of the photos from him, about a dozen in all, tossing them one by one on the table as she quickly went through them. "It's probably Marsha."

I wonder why she's not showing off her pink negligee…

She looked up, totally disgusted. "These must belong to Jock. No one else would have access to my attic or would even consider storing something like this up there without my knowledge." She tossed the last one on the table. "I wonder if he was using them to blackmail her."

Shane gave her a *duh* look.

"Well, that figures," she complained angrily. "Jock stores incriminating pictures in my attic with the most important section torn off." She picked up one showing the woman sitting with her knees pulled to her chest. "Look." Stephanie pointed to the left foot. "Her middle toe is crooked and there's a tiny scar where part of the toenail has been removed."

"I hadn't noticed that," Shane remarked as he studied the photo.

She playfully slugged his shoulder. "I wonder why!"

He smiled. "Now all we have to do is find a woman with a gimpy toe."

They laughed knowing that would probably never happen.

*   *   *

Five days later, on Friday, the email from Town and Country Life Insurance Company appeared in Stephanie's inbox on her phone. It was two days early! It must be a notice that her claim had been denied. She was on the clock at *Chloe's Couture* so she didn't have much time to read it on her break. She sat at a small table in their closet-sized breakroom and stared hard as her eyes scanned the text, absorbing the content.

Her claim had been accepted and was being processed. The company requested her bank information to deposit the funds within the next two weeks. The amount listed was a cool *five million dollars.*

It was a good thing she was sitting down because her head began to spin as heat climbed up the back of her neck. Her breath came in shallow pants. She set the phone on the table and placed her cold, sweaty hands over her hot cheeks. "Thank you, Jock," she whispered in a daze. "Thank you from the bottom of my heart."

She inhaled a deep breath. Five million dollars? *Ohmygosh…* How much money was that, really? She'd read once that a person could fit a million dollars into a paper grocery bag. That meant she had the equivalent of five grocery bags.

She laughed aloud, trying to imagine herself placing the brimming bags into her car as bundles of money spilled out, dropping on the ground.

She sobered, realizing she couldn't simply leave it in her checking account. She needed to do something with it—invest it somehow—but she had no clue where or how to start.

My dad, she thought, calming down. *I need to talk to my dad about this.*

By the time Stephanie left the boutique, she'd made a few decisions. She called her father on the walk to the transit shelter.

"Dad," she said breathlessly as soon as she heard his voice, "can you come over tonight? I've got something important that I need to talk to you about."

She heard the wariness in his voice as he asked her if she was in some kind of trouble. In other words, had she found herself pregnant with a dead guy's kid?

"No, Dad," she said seriously, but she was tempted to laugh. "I got some terrific news today, but I can't talk about it over the phone. I'm getting on the bus in a minute, and I'll be home in about a half-hour. Can you meet me there? Alone?"

He agreed.

* * *

Bob Jones sat in the driveway in his blue Ram pickup, waiting for Stephanie as she hurried through the side gate into her backyard. She signaled to him to come into the house and entered the back porch to go in through the kitchen. Hobbit stood on the other side of the door whining as she pulled out her keys and unlocked it. He rushed past her and out of the screen porch to greet her dad.

Bob stopped to pet the dog then walked swiftly into the kitchen and approached her wearing his usual outfit of Levi jeans and a short-sleeved striped shirt. Today the shirt was blue.

"What's going on, honey?" he said in his deep, but gentle voice. "What's your big news?"

She dumped her purse and her poncho on the table. "Jock left me his life insurance," she blurted without preamble. "It's in the millions."

Bob's grayish-green eyes widened. "How many?"

Like she did when she was a little girl, she held up her hand to indicate the amount with five fingers.

Her dad usually only swore when something made him mad, but a few choice words came out of his mouth today illustrating his utter amazement. He rubbed his hand across his thinning, light brown hair and chuckled. "That'll keep you in shoes for the rest of your life, but you'd better get an investment counselor to invest the rest of it."

She laughed, grateful that she had such a wise and wonderful father. "I plan to, Dad, as soon as it gets deposited into my bank account, but I also want to spend some of it on the house and I was hoping you would help me with that. I need to find a good contractor, but I have no idea where to start."

He looked around disapprovingly. "This old house needs a lot of work. Why don't you sell it and build yourself a new one?"

She shook her head. "Maybe someday, but not now. I like my little house and I don't want to leave Evelyn. She depends upon me to mow her lawn and shovel her sidewalk and take care of things that she can't do for herself."

"Are you sure?" He walked around, observing the interior. "This place needs new windows—"

"—insulation in the attic, an energy-efficient furnace, and a water heater," Stephanie added, finishing the sentence for him. "I'm aware of that because you've been telling me about it ever since I moved in. But the first thing I want is a new back porch with heat so I can sit out there all year around." *And enjoy my yard through every season.*

They spent three-quarters of an hour walking around the property, discussing potential improvements to the house, and by the time Bob left, they'd agreed that he would start getting bids immediately for the porch. The rest of the work she needed to get done would wait until next spring.

After he left, she went back into the house with Hobbit and kicked off her designer heels. "Yep," she said aloud, "I think I need a new pair of shoes." She smiled to herself, glowing inside over Jock's parting gift to her. "Maybe ten!"

Chapter Seventeen

On Saturday, the day of Jock's reception, Stephanie changed her outfit three times before she decided on an ankle-length, black dress with cap sleeves in a slinky knit fabric that hugged her curves. A matching cashmere shrug provided just enough warmth against the cool morning temperature. She slipped on a pair of black and silver animal print sandals with wedge heels for walking through the grass and brushed her thick, coppery hair, wearing it down. She fastened a thick gold chain around her neck and matching hoops in her ears. Both items were gifts from Jock.

Shane sauntered into her kitchen at noon wearing a pair of jeans and a white logo t-shirt under a yellow shirt printed with green palm leaves. His thick blond hair had been parted on the side and loosely combed. He stared at her through his pilot-style sunglasses. "Hey," he said as he stopped in front of her. "You look terrific."

"You look like Brad Pitt in *Once Upon a Time in Hollywood*."

His lips spread in a slow, sexy grin as his hands swept back the panels of his shirt and settled on his hips. "I've got his attitude today, too."

"Hmmm…" Stephanie said with a smile. "This should be an

interesting afternoon."

He pulled her close. "Maybe we should just skip the event at Valerie's and make our own little party."

She laughed and playfully pushed him away. "People are already arriving. I think we'd better get going."

The sooner we arrive, she thought sardonically, *the sooner we can leave.*

About a dozen people loitered around the makeshift bar under a milk-white tent in Valerie's backyard. Most of them were Jock's friends and closest business associates. The rest were Jock's family. The only people she didn't know were Shane's parents but he introduced her to them right away. Stephanie greeted everyone as she approached the bar. They greeted her back and expressed their condolences on the death of her boyfriend. All except Jock's father, Oliver. He acknowledged her presence with a nod but didn't utter a word. Did he somehow blame her for Jock's death?

Stu was busy behind the bar, the blender whirring loudly as he dipped several margarita glasses into a shallow bowl of salt. "Hey, hey, look who's here," he said over the grinding roar of the blender. A smudge of salt decorated the pocket of his bright red polo shirt. "Whatcha drinkin'?"

Shane ordered a beer. Stephanie settled for a Coke. It made no sense to start drinking yet. She had to keep her eyes and ears sharply tuned to these people.

Pat and Valerie emerged from the house holding large platters of cheese and crackers and veggie appetizers. They both halted when they saw her.

Shane slid his free arm around her shoulders. "Stephanie is my date."

Valerie smiled but neither woman said a word as they continued toward the buffet tables adorned in fall colors and decorated with pictures of Jock. They placed the dishes on the tables. Pat's perfume lingered in her wake like a vapor trail.

Stephanie sipped her Coke. *This reception might end sooner for me than I thought.*

By twelve-thirty, the tent was packed with people and the booze was flowing like water. Stephanie stood off to one side, feeling out of place as she observed the people imbibing around her and wondering how getting drunk honored Jock's memory. Oliver hushed the crowd for a few minutes to give a tribute to his late son and to propose a toast, but after that, the drinking commenced, and the atmosphere lightened considerably.

Rudy arrived fashionably late and proudly strolled through the crowd with Marsha on his arm like he was escorting Miss America. She wore a long, royal blue dress, a glittery white formal jacket, and a dazzling show of diamonds around her neck. Rudy had on a navy double-breasted jacket and white pants. They reminded her of Thurston Howell III and Ginger Grant on that old show, *Gilligan's Island.*

The thought made Stephanie laugh out loud. Those two had been shipwrecked, all right.

A team of caterers served the buffet at one-thirty and by that time, most people had consumed so much liquor they were starving. Fried chicken, potato salad, sliced ham sandwiches, coleslaw, chips, and an assortment of fruits and veggies were served.

Stephanie stood at the end of the food line, listening intently to multiple conversations going on around her while she waited her turn. She sensed someone come up behind her and turned to find Valerie sipping on a glass of white wine.

"Sorry about leaving you off the invitation situation list, kid," Valerie said honestly. "I'm glad you came anyway. I wanted to include you, but Pat nixed it."

"That's okay, Val." Stephanie shrugged. "I think she believes I'm a fortune hunter who seduced Jock and made off with his diamonds. I didn't, you know. I have no idea what he did with them, but I do know what he was *going* to do with them."

Valerie suddenly perked up. "What?"

"Build his own jewelry store," Stephanie whispered. "On France Avenue, not far from his condo."

Valerie stared at her, clearly stunned at the news. "He never said anything to me about that. Are you sure?"

Stephanie nodded. "I saw the plat map of the property he purchased."

Deep in thought, Valerie drained her glass and walked away.

"What's wrong with her?" Stephanie grumbled under her breath. "He didn't tell me, either."

She left the buffet line and walked over to the bar where Marsha and Rudy stood drinking martinis. Lunch could wait. It was time to stir the pot.

Marsha pinned her with a venomous look as she approached. "You've got a lot of nerve showing up here. I heard you weren't invited."

"Yes, I was," Stephanie replied smoothly. "I'm Shane's guest."

Marsha glared across the room where Shane having a conversation with Jock's sister, Amelia. "Your California beach bum. The guy who gets his clothes from the Goodwill store. He looks like the black sheep of the family."

"He's happy with his life. Are you?" Stephanie said slyly as her gaze shifted from Marsha to Rudy. "He can sleep at night because he doesn't have to worry about trying to get his hands on a stack of nude pictures or explain to the detectives what he was doing on Jock's boat the night Jock was murdered. How about you?"

Rudy's eyes hardened, glittering like the diamonds he so desperately wanted to get his hands on.

Marsha's face paled. She placed her hands over her stomach like she had all she could do to keep from throwing up the fancy martinis she'd been slugging down all afternoon. "Who told you about that?"

Stephanie gave her a smug smile. "Wouldn't you like to know?"

Rudy moved close, his bushy brows furrowing together. "If you know what's good for you, *Jones*, you'll keep your mouth shut about that night. About everything that doesn't concern you."

"Why?" She asked them. "Did one of you kill Jock? Or, was it a group effort? He double-crossed you both."

Rudy grabbed Marsha by the arm. "Don't answer that." He steered her away from the bar and into the crowd.

So, Stephanie thought triumphantly, *Marsha is worried about those pictures. Hmmm... I think I'm going to turn them over to Detective Garrett tonight.*

"Stephanie," Stu said from behind the bar, beckoning her with one finger to come and talk to him. "What's going on?" He pointed to a couple of men in her backyard walking around with a tape measure.

"Oh, that's my dad. He's getting bids today from a contractor." She smiled proudly. "I'm building a new back porch. A larger one that I can use all year round."

Stu watched the men, genuinely interested. "You're tearing off the old one and building a four-season porch? Sounds expensive."

"I've got the money," she announced loudly before she realized what she'd said. "Ah... I mean, my dad's paying for it."

That was partially true. In order to get the work started before it got too cold to pour concrete, they had agreed that Bob would pay the down payment and she would reimburse him when her insurance funds came through. But the damage had been done. It sounded like an excuse to cover her mistake.

Pat Tanner stopped talking in mid-sentence.

Stu's face darkened with doubt, giving her the notion that he thought the timing of her remodeling project was too unlikely of a coincidence to actually *be one*.

She caught Rudy's eye and tensed at the murderous look on his face.

He knows the money came from Jock's insurance…

She spun away, not in the mood to answer any more of Stu's nosy questions or put up with Rudy's dirty looks. She made her way toward Shane, who now stood talking to Valerie. "Let's get something to eat, Shane. Come on, Val. There's no line at the buffet."

At the buffet, they grabbed plates and silverware and proceeded to peruse their food choices. Valerie took her knife and mumbled something as she used it to pick through a silver chafing dish of barbequed ribs. Stephanie and Shane continued to fill their plates with delicious food, but Valerie suddenly set down her knife, left her half-filled plate on the table, and made a beeline to the bar to get another glass of wine from Stu.

They found a table and sat down to eat their lunch. Midway through their meal, Shane's phone chirped. He stopped eating and stared at the text, but instead of answering it, he shoved it into his pocket. Stephanie wondered what had caused him to become so tense, but figured it was a personal matter that he didn't want to discuss. Had Pat berated him for bringing her to the reception?

On the opposite side of the tent, Rudy was arguing with Marsha about how much she was drinking. Her voice became so shrill Oliver Tanner had to break them up and pull Marsha aside to calm her down.

After lunch was served, the bar closed, and people began to leave.

Rudy pulled Marsha to her feet and slipped his arm around her waist, walking her to his car. On the way out, she turned and flipped Stephanie the bird.

Stephanie turned away and grabbed a frosted brownie off the dessert table, unconcerned that she'd ruined Marsha's day. This luncheon was supposed to be a tribute to Jock's memory but instead, it had turned into a drunken free-for-all.

What a waste of time, she thought irritably. *I got to rattle Rudy's cage and cross-examine Marsha, but I still didn't get a confession out of her or Rudy. I can't wait to get home and enjoy the rest of my day.*

She and Shane said goodbye to Valerie and Jock's family. She chuckled with relief as Shane walked her back to her house. "Boy, am I glad that's over. I did learn one thing, though. Marsha got very nervous when I mentioned those headless pictures to her, and I think she would have admitted to me that they were hers if Rudy hadn't interfered."

"What?" Even though he replied right away, Shane sounded disinterested. His gaze was riveted on his phone.

She repeated her words, but he continued to stare at his phone.

At the back porch, he shoved it into his pocket and silently held the door for her. Something was wrong. She sensed the discomfort in his silence.

"What's going on?" she asked as they stood in the kitchen. "You look concerned. Did you learn something important at the reception?"

He exhaled a deep sigh and slid his arms around her waist as he gazed into her eyes. "I got a text from Dack's assistant. Dack has called a meeting tomorrow morning about our next production. "That means I have to catch a plane tonight back to L.A. It sounds like Dack is ready to get back to work so I don't know when I'll be back."

She stood quietly with his arms around her, not knowing what to say. She always knew this day would come, but never realized how much it would hurt to see him go. "That's great. I'm happy for you, but what about Jock's estate?"

"It's in the hands of his attorney until all the legal stuff gets sorted out. We'll be communicating regularly."

Though she tried, she couldn't stop her eyes from filling with tears. "We failed spectacularly as amateur detectives, didn't we? I don't regret it, though."

"I don't either. We gave it our best shot. That's all that matters." He lifted her chin to look into her eyes. "I'm going to miss you, Stephanie. I'll call you every day."

Maybe at first, she thought sadly, *but you'll get busy on the set and prettier women will distract you. It won't take long for you to forget me.*

As if he read her thoughts, he tightened his arms around her and kissed her deeply. She knew he didn't want to break her heart, but it truly felt like a kiss of goodbye. She gently pushed him away. "You'd better get going. You have a plane to catch."

He didn't move, as though reluctant to leave her. "Promise me you'll be careful, Stephanie. Jock's murderer is still out there—"

"Goodbye, Shane."

He got the message and nodded as he backed away, his deep blue eyes mirroring sadness. "Goodbye, Stephanie."

Shane Kingsley left by the kitchen door and never looked back.

Chapter Eighteen

Stephanie sat curled up on her sofa in a terry jogging suit with a soft blanket and a box of tissues, dabbing at the moisture in her eyes. A hot bath and a cup of cocoa hadn't helped her mood. A small sob escaped from her throat. Life was going to be really dull without Shane. Her heart ached with a hollowness that she hadn't experienced with Jock's passing.

It wasn't as if she was all alone. Besides her family, she had the girls in her book club. They were her besties—and she cherished their loyal friendship—but hanging out with them just wasn't the same as being with Shane. She'd never forget the lively dinners they shared in the Irish pub or the juicy burgers they devoured at the root beer stand, searching Jock's properties for clues, the heart-to-heart talks about their lives, and the passionate kiss they'd shared...

I've been through a lot lately, she ruminated with a sniffle. She rubbed her nose with a tissue. *Discovering Jock's body really shook me to the core, but Shane's constant encouragement was the one thing that kept me going. What will I do without him?*

Katie's no-nonsense voice echoed in her head. *Quit feeling sorry for yourself. Get up, count your blessings, and get busy!*

She sighed, knowing in her heart that Shane had the best of

intentions to stay in touch, but given his busy life in California, his enthusiasm for a long-distance relationship would soon wane. It wouldn't do her any good to mope over him. They had fun while it lasted, but that was that.

Hobbit jumped on the sofa and nudged her hand as though he, too, wanted her to stop fussing and be grateful for what she *did* have. "You're right, my little sweetie." She petted the top of his smooth head as she marveled over her newest blessings, all five million of them. It was still so hard to fathom. What would she do with all of that money?

She suddenly remembered what her grandma used to say. "To whom much is given, much is required."

Her hand stilled as she pondered what that meant. An impression filtered through her mind then it went straight to her heart. She'd seen an ad on television about a local hospital that treated seriously ill children and provided a temporary place for the parents to stay. Her heart swelled.

That's it, she thought, elated by the idea of helping children in need. *I'll set aside some of the money to do good for others...*

"The second thing is, I need to do something nice for Mom and Dad," she said aloud as she absently stroked Hobbit's soft fur. "They won't take any money, but they can't turn down a cruise to Alaska if I've already paid for it." Her dad had talked about visiting that place many times and going deep-sea fishing. Taking a cruise *anywhere* had been her mom's dream.

She slid off the sofa and set the tissue box on the coffee table. Her father had left her a copy of the bid for the construction work on the kitchen table with a note letting her know that the contractor wanted to start demolishing the porch in two days, so she needed to clean it out and move her things to the garage. Yessiree, she needed to get busy!

But as soon as she walked into the back porch the flowerbeds lining her backyard caught her undivided attention and she quickly got sidetracked by a terrific daydream. What if she completely redesigned her backyard and added flowers around her new porch?

"Yes!" Stephanie shouted as she went back into the kitchen to search for a pen and paper, feeling better already. She needed to make a drawing in detail of a new layout.

Unfortunately, the only pen she could find in her junk drawer was as dry as a bone. Frustrated, she threw it into the trash and dug into her purse, looking for the box holding *The Marilyn*. That pen was soooo heavy, but it was all she had…

She ventured outdoors with a small notebook and the pen in hand and got busy making a preliminary drawing of her idea.

"Hey there," a familiar voice echoed over her shoulder mixed with sandalwood perfume.

Startled, Stephanie screamed as she whirled around for a showdown with Pat Tanner over showing up at the reception uninvited but found Valerie standing behind her instead. The notebook and the diamond pen went flying out of her hands. "Oh! You scared me." She placed her hands over her heart, taking a deep breath. "I was so busy working on my new project that I didn't hear you come into the yard."

"Sorry about that," Valerie said softly. She wore flip-flops, a pair of denim leggings, and a red polo shirt, the same one Stu had worn that afternoon. Her shoulder-length blonde hair looked tousled, as though she'd just crawled out of bed. "I saw you wandering around over here sketching notes in your book and I wondered what you were up to. Making plans? Stu says you've come into some money…"

"I'm exploring new designs for my flower garden because my dad is building me a new porch," Stephanie said quickly. "He's taking care of *everything*."

The dubious look in Valerie's eyes indicated she didn't believe it.

The pen had fallen between their feet. Stephanie reached down to retrieve it and the notebook from the ground. "At first, I thought you were Pat Tanner. Why are you wearing her perfume?"

"I'm not," Valerie replied curtly. "I introduced her to this brand. I can't help it if she practically bathes in it."

Bent at the waist, Stephanie froze as her gaze focused on a small scar on the middle toe of Valerie's right foot where a sliver of toenail was missing. The discovery caught her off guard, stunning her. She swallowed hard and straightened quickly, struggling to conceal her shock. "Wh—where's Stu?"

"He had too much to drink this afternoon." Valerie's lips pursed as though she found his fondness for liquor annoying. "He's sprawled across my bed, sleeping it off."

Stu had stood behind the bar knocking back shots of whiskey as he mixed drinks for the guests. Stephanie had never seen him consume that much liquor before. What had caused him to get so drunk today of all days? Guilt perhaps?

Valerie's gaze zeroed in on the pen. "Are those real diamonds?"

"Um…yeah," Stephanie replied, distracted by the fact that the nude pictures Jock had hidden in her attic—minus the head—were of Valerie. *Jock and Valerie were having an affair?* She couldn't imagine… But then, how else would he have obtained those provocative images?

There was just one problem. Marsha had practically admitted they were hers! Had Jock taken pictures of her, too? If so, where were they? Maybe he had destroyed them. Or…maybe they were already in the hands of Detective Garrett.

She held out the pen, her mind spinning in a kaleidoscope of emotions. "It's covered in De Beers diamonds." Though she tried not to reveal the hurt and betrayal that squeezed her heart, an unmistakable note of sadness slipped through anyway. "Do you want to see it up close?"

Valerie took *The Marilyn* and examined it, rolling the heavy tool between her thumb and forefingers as though trying to imagine what it would feel like to own such an extravagant gift. "This thing is exquisite." She looked up. "It must be worth a small fortune. Enough to pay for your porch and more."

"I guess so." Stephanie shrugged. "I've never really given it much thought. It's just another piece of jewelry to me."

"I find that hard to believe," Valerie responded wryly. "For someone who supposedly doesn't care all that much for fine jewelry, you sure own a lot of it."

Valerie's directness puzzled her. *How would you know how much jewelry I own?*

"Jock didn't tell me what the value was when he gave it to me and at the time, I didn't think to ask," she replied. "He was desperate to convince me not to break up with him."

"He always talked his way back into your life by bribing you with diamonds, but it didn't last, did it?" Valerie laughed. "Tough luck, kid. You should have learned a long time ago that it never would with him."

Really? Stephanie thought, becoming irritated at Valerie's smug superior attitude. *She has some nerve. Who is the real loser here? The rich redhead or the headless ho?*

"No, it didn't last for long. He betrayed me again and again," Stephanie countered as a slow burn began to cloud her judgment. "Of course, you know about that *intimately*, don't you?"

Valerie's eyes narrowed. "What do you mean?"

She thrust out her hand, indicating she wanted the pen back. "I found the pictures, Val." Random facts began to fall into place, making her realize that the truth had been staring her in the face all along. "They were stashed in my attic, the one place you missed when you burglarized my house."

Valerie's chiseled features hardened into a stone-faced mask. "I don't know what you're talking about."

"Yes, you do." Stephanie tried to grab the pen back, but Valerie jerked her hand away. "You were a willing participant. You enjoyed posing for the pictures that Jock took of you *in the nude.*"

"Wrong," Valerie countered with a quick laugh. "You saw pictures of a headless woman. You have no proof that it's me."

"I'll bet Stu will recognize you when I show the stack to him," Stephanie shot back. "And I plan to do it as soon as he wakes up. He'll forget all about his hangover when he sees the evidence of your sordid little orgy with his best friend. He'll cut you off in more ways than one when I show him what you've been doing behind his back. And mine!"

"He's never going to see those images," Valerie said in a low, threatening tone. "Because we're going to make an exchange." She held up *The Marilyn.* "No pictures, no pen. Understand?"

Stephanie shoved her notebook into the back of her waistband and placed her hands on her hips, surprised at how quickly Valerie tried to get the upper hand once her secret had been exposed. "Keep it. I don't care about that stupid pen," she said, calling Valerie's bluff. "I'd rather see you get what's coming to you."

She meant that she would find satisfaction in telling Stu what a fool he'd been to believe that his ex-wife still cared about him, but the feral glare in Valerie's eyes pulled her up short. There was obviously more at stake than the pictures. But what else was there? Unless...

She folded her arms and glared back. "You're the woman Pat Tanner thought would make the perfect wife for her son, aren't you? The way she treated you at the funeral made her preference clear. You relished all of the attention you were getting, but I'll bet it was driving you nuts knowing that had Jock lived, he was going to propose *to me.*"

"He would have never gone through with it, especially with a ditzy redhead like you," Valerie retorted. "He wasn't the marrying kind."

"That's what you want to believe, but we both know it isn't true," Stephanie argued. "I have the hand-written copy of his new will, the one he never got the chance to finish. He named me *as his wife*—in charge of everything."

Valerie's jaw tightened, her eyes glittering over having the truth flung in her face. She had been used by Jock just like she had used him. "That means you're sitting on a pile of diamonds," she said in a low, suspicious voice. "You're good at playing the innocent one, but you don't fool me. You've had them all along, haven't you?"

Something in the way Valerie accused her gave her an ominous vibe but she refused to let the woman's threatening tone get to her. "Why do you care?"

"Don't play games with me." Valerie retaliated with a hard shove, knocking Stephanie backward. "Jock proposed to buy my silence when I discovered he was stockpiling them. He owes me for not telling Rudy how he was robbing his own store. Now that he's gone, I'm making some changes. You're going to hand over those pictures and *all* of the diamonds. If all you care about is the money, I'll make it worth your while."

Stephanie recovered her footing. "Uh-huh."

Valerie's aggressiveness astonished her. She'd never seen this side of the woman—her so-called friend, but she stood her ground. "I don't care about the money. I'm giving the pictures to Stu." She stabbed the air with one finger. "You're going to pay dearly for sleeping with my boyfriend. As for the diamonds…" She shook her head. "I don't know where they are, and I've given up trying to find them."

"Don't lie to me. You've got them stashed around here somewhere and I want them *now*." Valerie shoved her again, this time much harder. The action frightened her, causing her to stumble backward. She fell against the cement birdbath, knocking the bowl off its pedestal. Water spilled everywhere as it hit the ground. In a panic, she grabbed for the shepherd's hook and missed, pulling the bee bowl out of the chain that held it. She landed on the wet ground at the same time the bowl fell on the edge of the birdbath, breaking into several pieces. Dozens of pebbles flew out of the bowl and scattered among the rosebushes.

She gasped, ready to cry. "Oh, my gosh! My bee bowl! Look what you did!"

Valerie pulled the cap off the pen and raised one arm, aiming at Stephanie's heart with the sharp tip. "I could care less about your stupid bowl. Things are going to get worse if you don't quit whining and start cooperating!"

Carrying on behind her back with Jock was bad enough, but *nobody* destroyed her garden and got away with it. Nobody! Valerie had to be the one who'd ransacked her house and destroyed her garden looking for the diamonds. Who else would have known that Evelyn would be away from home that evening? Who else would have had reason to think she'd hid them under the bushes?

Seething, Stephanie sprang to her feet and charged toward Valerie, grabbing the sharp end of the pen with both hands. The time for trying to reason with this witch *was over*. "I'll tell you what *I* think happened between you and Jock. You were so upset when he dumped you that you threatened to tattle to me about your affair, but he one-upped you with the pictures and said he'd give them to Stu if you didn't back off." She refused to let go, struggling to get the pen away from her attacker. "You went to see him on the boat after dark and he refused to hand over the prints. So, you stabbed him and wiped your prints off the knife, thinking you'd snatch them and get out of there before anyone saw you, but you couldn't find them."

Valerie grabbed her by the hair. "You can't prove a thing!"

She managed to pull away, leaving Valerie with a handful of

long, coppery strands. "I already have," she said rubbing a sore spot on her head where her hair had been ripped out. "The pictures will prove you had an affair with Jock at the same time you were sleeping with Stu. I've also got a card you gave him confirming one of your liaisons—with your fingerprints on it. Now that he knows what to look for, I'm sure it won't be difficult for Detective Garrett to retrace your movements and find people who can place you at the scene that night."

"You'll never get the chance to pull it off, Stephanie." Valerie stuck her foot behind Stephanie's heel, tripping her backward onto the grass again. "Poor, dumb redhead. I have no idea what he saw in you. Jock came to a bad end, and you will too." She stared at the sharp tip of the pen. "It's not as effective as a steak knife, but it will do."

How did she know Jock was killed with a steak knife? Stephanie smiled inwardly, knowing she'd just caught Valerie in the one lie that could incriminate her. The cops had deliberately kept that information from the public.

Valerie leaned over Stephanie's prone body with the pen in her raised hand. "Everybody knows you've got two left feet. It'll be easy to convince people that you tripped and fell—impaling yourself on your own pen."

Not if I can help it…

Stephanie tried to roll out of the way, but Valerie's fist came down quickly, stabbing her in the upper arm. She cried out at the sharp pain and raised her other hand, struggling to push Valerie away when suddenly they were both deluged with a heavy spray of water. Valerie screamed and tried to shield her body from the onslaught, giving Stephanie an opening to roll out of the way and scramble to her feet.

Evelyn stood on her side of the chain link fence spraying Valerie with a garden hose on full blast.

"Hmph!" Her short, chunky arms pointed the hose nozzle at Valerie's face as if it was a bullseye. "Maybe next time she'll think twice before excluding me from her invitation list!"

* * *

"Ahhh!" Stephanie cried with a loud groan as she pulled the pen from her bleeding arm. By the time Evelyn turned off the hose, she and Valerie were both sopping wet and shivering in the late afternoon air.

"Stephanie, you're bleeding!" Evelyn cried. "I'll hold her down so you can get away." She held up the hose and turned it on Valerie again. "Hurry!"

Art Gale appeared at the side gate, his eyes widening at the crimson blood covering Stephanie's clothes. "You're hurt! What happened?" he shouted as he burst through and ran toward the women.

"She tried to kill me!" Stephanie cried and pointed an accusing finger at Valerie.

Valerie turned and ran toward her house, but Art quickly caught up with her and restrained her, pinning her arms behind her back. "Get your hands off of me!" she screamed.

He held onto her tightly. "You're not going anywhere, lady, until the cops get here!" He turned to Evelyn. "Call 9-1-1!"

"Art, I'm *so* glad you're here," Stephanie said breathlessly as she clutched her arm and collapsed into a lawn chair.

"Shane called me on his way to the airport and asked me to keep an eye on you tonight," Art said, his voice booming above Valerie's protests and threats. "He was worried that you might run into trouble once people knew he was gone. I was sitting in my car watching you two talking when Valerie attacked you. I came as fast as I could!"

"I'll get you for this!" Valerie said in a voice so low the words came out as a hiss as Art bound her wrists with a large zip tie. He dragged her over to a lawn chair and forced her to sit down. "You have no reason to hold me against my will. I have rights! When Stu wakes up and sees what you're doing to me, he'll get me out of here. You just wait and see."

Evelyn stood in the kitchen window, talking on the phone and gesturing wildly with her free hand. When she hung up, she came back outdoors. "They're on their way. The police station is only a half-mile from here."

A siren immediately pierced the air. Stephanie barely had time to fill Art in on the details of what brought on Valerie's attack when a squad car pulled up in front of the house. An officer came into the backyard and immediately took control of the situation.

Suddenly, another squad car arrived. Then an ambulance pulled up to the house. Within minutes, her backyard was overrun with policemen and EMTs. A large group of curious onlookers congregated in the alley, watching the commotion. Some people were filming the episode on their phones.

Evelyn had covered Stephanie's shoulders with a blanket to keep her warm as she waited for medical personnel to arrive. Hobbit had been taken into the house to prevent him from causing a ruckus by barking at everyone. Valerie sat in the back of a squad car, wet and angry, demanding to speak to her attorney.

When Stu finally emerged from Valerie's house, shirtless, he stood on the back steps, looking baffled. "What's going on? What's with all of the sirens?" He saw Valerie sitting in the back of a squad car parked in Stephanie's driveway and ran to her. "What's going on, Val? Why are you sitting in the squad car?" He tried to open the car door and free her when a pair of police officers intercepted him. One of the officers took him aside and attempted to explain to him what had happened, but he refused to listen. "You people are crazy! My wife wouldn't try to kill anybody! She's a *good* person."

Stephanie turned away before his outburst tempted her to blurt out the truth. Stu would find out soon enough what kind of a woman he'd married and divorced. She didn't want to be around when he learned that

Valerie had slept with his best friend and then murdered Jock to cover up her affair.

Detective Garrett arrived. After speaking to his officers, he approached her, staring at her bandaged arm. "Ms. Jones, are you alright?"

She nodded and filled him in on the details, including the evidence she and Shane had discovered. "I never would have guessed that Valerie murdered my boyfriend," she said, still shocked by the revelation. "But the evidence I've found doesn't lie. I've got the pictures that Jock took of her. When I confronted her about being on Jock's boat the night he was murdered, she said that Jock had been stabbed with a steak knife. Both Evelyn and I witnessed it. Then Val tried to kill me because I denied having the diamonds and I wouldn't give her the photographs that proved she had a motive to murder him." Stephanie held up *The Marilyn*, showing him the sharp tip. "With this."

Detective Garrett whistled as his gaze beheld the dazzling instrument. Even in the waning light and covered with blood, its exquisite beauty shone through. "Are those real diamonds?"

"Yes, it was a gift from Jock," Stephanie said soberly. "When the officers asked me what happened, they insisted they needed it for evidence, but I promised Jock I'd always protect it, so I don't want to give it up. And in all the commotion, I've lost the cap." She glanced around in frustration. "It has to be around here somewhere, but I can't find it."

He surveyed the area, swishing the toe of his shoe through the grass. "It couldn't have gone far." He walked over to her flower garden and examined the birdbath. The wide bowl had been knocked off its pedestal. The broken bee bowl and a dozen pebbles rested inside it. "Is this where the attack happened?"

Stephanie followed him. "Yes, that's where Valerie knocked me backward. I fell on top of the birdbath and toppled the bowl." Luckily, the notebook she'd shoved into the back of her waistband had prevented her from hurting her back when she fell against it. "I can put the birdbath back together, but the bee bowl is beyond repair. It was another gift from Jock."

"I'm sorry to hear that." Detective Garrett stared at the broken pieces. "My wife has one of those bee things, too." He palmed a couple of the pebbles. "It looks like the rocks are scattered all over your garden. That's a shame."

She responded with a tired shrug. "Oh, well. I'll pick them up tomorrow. Right now, I just want to find the cap to my pen."

The detective paused, rolling the pebbles in his palm as he examined them. "Where did you get these?"

She picked up a handful of the colorful rocks and dropped them into the birdbath. "They came in the kit with the bee bowl."

He held up a rock to examine it closer. "These are different than the ones my wife has. Hers are more like little glass marbles." His phone rang. He tossed the rocks into the birdbath, pulled his phone from his pocket, and turned away to answer his call.

A tall figure stood at the gate, trying to convince the officer standing guard to let him come into the yard.

Stephanie sprang from her chair, knocking it backward. "Shane!" She hobbled over to him. "It's okay, officer. He's my—" She halted, wondering how Shane would describe their relationship. Were they merely friends or had he come back because he wanted to be more than that?

The officer stepped aside and opened the gate. Shane came toward her, his face stricken at the sight of so much blood on her clothes. "Stephanie…are you alright? I got here as fast as I could. When I heard you were hurt, I was so worried about you I thought my heart would burst!" He held out his arms, gingerly cupping her face with his hands.

"All I want to do right now is take you in my arms and hold you so tight, but I don't want to hurt you." He glanced down at her bandaged arm. "Did they give you something to ease the pain?"

She smiled, her heart melting at the tenderness in his voice. "Yeah, they did. It still hurts like crazy, but it's not as bad as it looks. The stab wound wasn't deep enough to cause a serious injury. Did Art call you?"

His gaze held hers. "The moment I saw his number ringing on my phone, I knew something bad had happened. I ran out of the airport while I was talking to him and grabbed the first cab I could find to get back here."

"You warned me to be careful," Stephanie said somberly. "I'm sorry, Shane. I should have listened to you."

"You couldn't have known that Valerie meant you harm," he said as he placed his palm on the small of her back. "Our investigation didn't uncover anything connected with her until we found the photographs. Even then, we didn't know they were of her."

"Actually, it did," Stephanie insisted. "Everything pointed to her, only we didn't realize it. The perfume we smelled everywhere we went belonged to Val—not Pat. It was her nightie under the bed, not Marsha's. The monogrammed socks in Jock's locker were a gift from her. The note in his windbreaker pocket was from her, too, but none of those facts fell into place until I saw the scar on her middle toe. That's when I suspected she had a motive to murder Jock. But then we started arguing and she let slip the one thing that only we knew. The murder weapon was a steak knife."

She glanced toward Valerie's house where Stu paced the sidewalk, talking furiously to someone—most likely his lawyer—on the phone. "When Jock told Val he was going to marry me," she continued, "it must have made her pretty mad. She didn't deny it when I accused her of threatening him to tell me about their affair. But I think then Jock retaliated and said he'd show the pictures to Stu. She realized she would lose Stu as well if he ever saw those nude images, so she murdered Jock to get them back."

Shane shook his head. "She must have been *really* mad when she couldn't find them."

"She knew about the diamonds, too," Stephanie added. "Jock had bribed her to stay quiet, but he hadn't paid her yet. She's the one who ransacked my house and dug up my garden. She knew how nosy Evelyn is, but she also knew when Evelyn wouldn't be home."

Shane gently pulled her off to one side. "I came back because I needed to know you were okay." He paused, dipping his head low to whisper in her ear. "But most of all, I realized that my life would never be the same if I lost you. I didn't know how I would manage without you because I love you, Stephanie."

Her knees went weak, and they would have buckled had Shane's arm not held her up. She wanted to slide her arms around him and hold him close, but her arm hurt too much to raise it. Instead, she slid her free arm around him, nestling her uninjured shoulder in the crook of his arm as she pressed her cheek against the warmth of his chest. "I felt the same way tonight when you left, as though the bottom had fallen out of my world, Shane, because I love you, too."

He smiled then kissed her deeply, filling her with a burst of happiness that made her forget her pain—all of it, not just the physical injury she'd suffered today. Everything she'd gone through with Jock, his parents, and Valerie didn't matter anymore. She'd embarked on a new beginning in so many ways.

Detective Garrett approached them. "I hate to interrupt you lovebirds, but I have something to show you." He held up his phone and placed one of the pebbles from the bee bowl behind it. A screen suddenly appeared, showing a picture of the pebble in his palm, and accompanying text identifying it as a diamond.

Stephanie blinked in disbelief. *What?* She looked up. "How did you do that?"

"I downloaded a gemstone discovery app," he said with great interest. "The app scans the rock and identifies what kind it is. It says this one is actually a rough diamond. We'll have to get confirmation from a professional, of course, but I'm certain we're looking at the real thing." He held it up to the light. "This is a white one, but there's a whole pile of rocks over there in different shades and I'll bet they're all diamonds." He gestured toward the flower garden. "We checked the pedestal of the birdbath. It's hollow. And filled with more of those little rocks." He smiled happily. "I guess we now know where Mr. Tanner was storing his gems."

A uniformed officer approached them. "Sir, while we were collecting the rocks, we found this…" He held up the diamond cap to *The Marilyn*.

Stephanie let out a sigh of relief as she took the cap and put it back on *The Marilyn* where it belonged. Then she began to laugh uncontrollably.

Everyone was right. She'd had the diamonds all along.

Epilogue

October 31st

Stephanie stood in front of the full-length mirror fastened to the closet door in her bedroom, making last-minute adjustments to her costume. She'd decided to wear a Roaring 20s flapper dress for her neighborhood block party. The black sequined chemise was short with a silky fringe stitched to the V-shaped hem. She'd purchased a short dark wig, T-strap shoes, and a long string of pearly beads to wear around her neck. She added a pendant on a short chain. It was one of the raw diamonds that had fallen out of the bee bowl the night the bowl had broken.

She'd found it in the grass a week after the police had taken all of the stones away and she had immediately called Detective Garrett. He told her to keep it as a way to remember Jock and said he'd already forgotten their conversation. She'd left the pinkish-purple stone in its natural state and had it wire-wrapped in thin gold wire.

She'd invited her book club to the party and told them to meet her at the small park two blocks from her house at six o'clock for the potluck buffet. All of the girls had plans but Katie and Inga had confirmed they would meet her there for a quick bite to eat.

Vera had prepared barbequed meatballs in a slow cooker for her to bring and she'd also purchased decorated cookies from the bakery. Earlier that afternoon, Evelyn had taken Stephanie's food along with her own slow cooker filled with sauerkraut and short ribs down to the park to help the ladies who were setting up the tables and organizing everything. Besides the buffet, there would be a nighttime craft fair, activities for the kids, and a local band that had volunteered to provide music. Everyone was to provide their own beverages.

The old schoolhouse clock in her living room chimed six times. Excited to get going, she finished dabbing cherry red lipstick on her lips to form a "cupid's bow" and hurried to gather her black wool shawl. The evening would be cool, but there would be several steel firepits positioned around the park to keep people warm. She fed the dog and left the house.

The girls were already there when she arrived, sitting together at a picnic table covered with an orange tablecloth near the temporary stage and munching on appetizers. Strings of Halloween lights were strung around the park, giving it a festive glow. A carved jack 'o lantern sat in the center of every table. Small paper bag luminaries were placed along the sidewalks leading to the craft fair and the buffet. Evergreen Park was filled with families in a variety of costumes.

Katie waved her over. She wore a black witch costume with a large pointed hat. "Are you by yourself?"

"Of course." Baffled by the question, Stephanie glanced around. "Both of you are already here."

Inga pointed to the empty seat across from her. "Come and sit down." She had on a long blue dress like Princess Elsa from the Disney movie *Frozen*. Her ice-blonde hair flowed freely about her shoulders. She slid a bowl of chips and dip across the table. "Have some, but be warned—they're addicting."

Stephanie grabbed a cocktail plate and filled it with wavy potato chips and a cheesy dip. She noticed that the girls had made up another small plate of chips and dip. "Who is the extra plate for?"

"For me."

Recognizing the rich, deep timbre of his voice, she twisted in her seat. "Shane!"

He stood under the soft lights wearing a dark pinstripe suit with a white shirt and suspenders. A black Fedora was pulled low over his eyes.

She jumped to her feet and flew into his arms laughing with delight. "Shane, what are you doing here? I thought you were supposed to be on the set this weekend to start filming."

He kissed her and held her tight. "The film is on hold. Dack's shoulder isn't getting any better so he's decided to retire from acting and start directing instead."

Since they talked on the phone nearly every day, that surprised her but the news meant they might have a few days together. "Does that mean you're out of a job?"

He cocked his head to one side. "No, there are other jobs, but I've worked with Dack on all of his films since I got into the business. I hope to work with him again one day." He took her by the hand. "Let's get something to eat. I'm starving.

"I parked in your driveway. I hope you don't mind," he said as they walked holding hands. I wanted to see your new porch. It's beautiful. How do you like it?"

"I love it!" she exclaimed. "I sit out there every morning and enjoy my coffee."

"I noticed the Realtor's sign in Valerie's front yard as I was walking over here," Shane said as they arrived at the long, white food tent. "Now that she has been charged with Jock's murder, I guess she isn't going to need it any longer." He pointed toward *the Ghouls and Goblins* craft fair—brightly lit tents containing handmade items for sale. "Hey, is that a gypsy wagon?"

Stephanie whirled around. Sure enough. At the far end of the row of tents sat a dark brown "cottage-style" coach with a bow top and intricately carved scrollwork in orange and gold covering the front. Above the entrance, a sign hung under a small light that read *Fortune Teller*.

It was the same wagon she'd visited at the James J. Hill Days celebration. She grimaced, remembering Esme, the gypsy who'd given her the dark fortune. She still recalled it:

"I implore you, beware of this warning,

a death occurred before morning.

Your life is in danger, watch out for the stranger,

dark days ahead are dawning…"

Unfortunately, every word of it had turned out to be true, even the warning about the stranger—which was Valerie, the neighbor who had a dark side that even her husband didn't know about.

Shane began to pull her toward the wagon. "Come on. Let's get our fortunes told. Won't that be a hoot on Halloween?"

She pulled back. "Absolutely not!" She could think of a lot of words to describe what kind of an experience it was and *hoot* wasn't among them.

He looked baffled. "Why not? It'll be fun!"

It'll be the worst mistake you ever made…

She needed to change the subject—and fast. There was something important she wanted to tell him anyway and now seemed like the right time to do it. "How would you like to go on a cruise to somewhere exotic?" she blurted. "Or take a trip to Europe?"

Shane laughed. "Of course! Wouldn't anybody? If they had the money, that is."

She looked up at him. "What if I told you that money isn't a problem?"

He laughed again. "Right. Who died and left you a fortune…" The word stalled on his lips as his eyes widened with shock. "You mean…Jock…left you money? How? You weren't in his will."

Stephanie slid her arm around his. "Let's get something to eat and I'll tell you all about it."

She suddenly couldn't wait to tell him about her inheritance. She couldn't wait to begin planning her future—with him.

The End

A note from Denise…

Thank you so much for reading **Dark Fortune.** If you'd like to know more about me or my other books, visit my website at

https://www.deniseannettedevine.com

More Books by Denise Devine

Christmas Stories
Merry Christmas, Darling
A Christmas to Remember
A Merry Little Christmas
A Very Merry Christmas - Hawaiian Holiday Series

~*~

Sweet Romance
The Encore Bride
Lisa – Beach Brides Series
Ava – Perfect Match Series
Della – Enchanted Island Series

~*~

Moonshine Madness Series - Historical Suspense/Romance
The Bootlegger's Wife – Book 1
Guarding the Bootlegger's Widow – Book 2
The Bootlegger's Legacy – Book 3

~*~

Charlotte Van Elsberg Mystery Series
The Nightengale Detective Agency – *Coming Soon!*

~*~

West Loon Bay Series – Small Town Romance
Small Town Girl – Book 1
Brown-Eyed Girl – Book 2
Country Girl – Book 3 - *Coming Soon!*

~*~

Christmas in West Loon Bay Series– Small Town Romance
Once Upon a Christmas – Book 1
Mistletoe and Wine – Book 2

~*~

Cozy Mystery

Unfinished Business

Dark Fortune

~ Girl Friday Cozy Series ~

Shot in the Dark – Book 1

The Accidental Detective – **Coming Soon!**

~*~

Forever Yours Series - Inspirational romance

Always is not Forever – Book 1

This Time Forever – Book 2

Want more? Read the first chapter of my novels or get my complete book list at:

https://deniseannette.blogspot.com

~*~

Audiobooks Galore!

Do you like audiobooks? Many in the list above are available in audio!
Check out Denise's website for links to each audiobook.

https://www.deniseannettedevine.com

Narrated by Lorana L. Hoopes

Monthly sales!